The Boy with the Knife

G. Malavan

Published by New Generation Publishing in 2022
Copyright © G. Malavan 2022

First Edition

The author asserts the moral right under the Copyright, Designs and Patents Act 1988 to be identified as the author of this work.

All Rights reserved. No part of this publication may be reproduced, stored in a retrieval system or transmitted, in any form or by any means without the prior consent of the author, nor be otherwise circulated in any form of binding or cover other than that which it is published and without a similar condition being imposed on the subsequent purchaser.

Paperback ISBN: 978-1-80369-398-9
Hardback ISBN: 978-1-80369-399-6
Ebook ISBN: 978-1-80369-400-9

www.newgeneration-publishing.com

New Generation Publishing

Contents

Intro 1
Jason 3
Doug Smith 5
Luke 7
Jason 8
Luke 10
Doug Smith 10
Luke 11
Doug's date with fate 12
Luke 12
Justice 12
Jason 14
Luke 14
Jason 14
Luke 16
Nightmares 16
Three months 17
Luke 17
Dave Samson, "The Priest" 18
The priest 19
Jason 20
The next day 20

- Dave Samson 21
- Luke 22
- Dave Samson 22
- Jason 24
- Luke 25
- Eeny, meeny, miny, moe… 26
- Wrap up 27
- Jason 29
- Police report: 30
- Mason 31
- Jason 32
- Silence 33
- The nightmare 33
- Luke 35
- Richard Sams 37
- Visiting Sams 37
- Richard Sams 42
- Happy Place 43
- Room 616 49
- Planning 55
- Jason 55
- Luke 57
- Jason 58
- The week away 59
- The first night 61
- Monday to Thursday 64
- Friday 66

The trip	69
Flight	71
Haiti	76
Second day	83
Process	87
Breakfast	91
Jason	93
Weeks later	93
Toby	94
Jason	96
Laura	97
Luke	98
Congress Plaza Hotel	99
The invite	100
The beginning of the end	101
Dinner	103
The day of the night	105
Last dinner	111
Room 616	113
The ball	124
Epilogue	126

This book is dedicated to every child abused in the name of greed, corruption and negligence.

What is wrong with you?
Don't you know they look up to you?
This beautiful wonder you tried to destroy,
Now filled with fear, no trust, no joy.
Innocence gone - forever shattered
You seem to think it never mattered.
This child should never have been a part of the evil inside your heart.

(Lady Kira, 2009, *BW Child Abuse Awareness Challenge)*

Intro

Jason could smell the fresh blood dripping off the knife in the child's hand. The stench seemed to grow with each breath. The frosty morning, or perhaps it was the lack of clothes on the boy's body, had made him turn a surreal color. Making him look almost see- through, as if he were a part of the dim blue forest surrounding him as if he'd played a crucial part in the battle of night and day.

However, he knew better, the eyes of the boy did not show any signs of breaking into dawn. His eyes not only possessed a coldness but also a rage. A fuming rage, an anger that would not have been believed if not seen. His hollow, dark eyes seemed like a deep black hole that would drown you in an instant in its endless emptiness. The boy slowly moved his head from side to side, almost like an old movie, cut up, hacked, torn, badly put together, keeping the constant eye contact, back and forth. Standing there with his ripped dirty clothes stained by blood, fear and shame he starts shaking. The urge to reach out and wipe his drowned cheeks becomes overwhelming but Jason knows better. He knows what is coming, as much as he wishes that it would not come… it always did, and it always shook him to his core.

The scream. The scream that always put an end to this dream, like it had done for most nights for the past six months, Jason woke up cold, sweaty and fed up, like every other night.

He had come to the end of his sanity wishing that the dreams would end or just end him. Whichever came first he would welcome with open arms.

Jason

If you asked him how those dreams had started, he would've just shrugged his shoulders. It was almost as if these dreams had always been with him, that's how familiar the dream was. At the same time, he could not tell who this child was, nor what the meaning of this dream was, or why he kept having the same dream over and over again.

Jason turned around, the glimpse of the alarm clock confirming what he suspected, 4:30 a.m., Always the same time for the past six months. Sleepless nights had taught him that there was no purpose in going back to sleep. He had spent hours upon hours in the past six months trying to go back and sleep but with no luck. What happened every night instead would be him just getting more and more frustrated and angry at the world and eventually he had just given into waking up early every morning.

As he rolled out of bed, he kicked his work papers on the floor. If there was any point in his life that Jason was happy to be in the police force, it would be at these godforsaken hours when the world would be asleep, yet his mind was working overtime. He bent down to pick up the most recent case, when a picture of the victim fell out: fifty-six, Caucasian male, married, two children, a mortgage, worked in the bank, the only thing missing was a dog and you would have had your picture-perfect family.

The victim had been missing for two weeks before a runner had found his body. Whatever was left of the body was not much to look at, the guy had truly upset someone, and someone had finally had their payback.

Despite a successful career at a very young age, Jason struggled with these crimes. He could never understand the violence and hatred that normal people had the ability to carry around. A person who could be someone's brother, sister, mother, father or friend could in a blink of an eye do something unforgivable, just like that in an instant. The years had taught Jason that eventually everything and everyone had a price, and in the wrong circumstances, everyone seemed to have one end currency. There was no doubt in his mind that killings like this one were personal, not random.

The body had been marked, disfigured. The genitals had been torn off, the head cut from ear to ear, the eyes gouged out and very carefully put down on the ground next to a bloody picture of the victim's family. The body had been left to make sure the message was loud and clear and most importantly not missed.

Doug Smith

He had the strange, exciting feeling within – knowing what he did was an unforgivable crime did not take away from his thrill. His excitement had consumed him, it always did.

The constant hunger for the excitement was what had led him to the sad state that he found himself in.

He had been aware of his obsession from an early age. He also very quickly realized what he felt and hungered for was not accepted in his society. He had tried to curb his thirst by establishing what would be classified as a "normal family" in society's eyes, but here he was in his fifties with his urge leading his every step, and plan, consuming his every thought.

He had tried, he really had tried, and yes there were times when he caught a glimpse of his children and felt a slight shame, even worry, but that was quickly pushed aside in his mind to a dark corner where he justified his actions so that he could carry on living with his filthy soul.

He knew if his secret ever came out his life would be over, but so far, he must have done well as no one had ever implied anything or even questioned him. Years of keeping it quiet and mastering his needs had enabled him to carry on. He could remember the first time he became aware of his feelings. It was indeed much earlier than when other children have started being aware of their hormones. Boys and girls exploring the opposite sex, sometimes the same sex, for Doug it was different from the very start. His hunger and weakness for younger children had started then, he had managed to stay in line with a few mishaps here and there but was lucky enough to not get caught.

When he was looking for his next victim, he knew exactly what he was looking for. Girl or boy didn't matter, age mattered. Age always mattered. It mattered the most. He wanted them young and clean, as if their purity could wash away all his sins, all the sick thoughts, all the sick things he had done in his past. All the little lives he had destroyed did not matter, *he* mattered, what he *wanted* mattered the most. He had to silence his hunger, however, the more he had the more his hunger increased. His last victim two years ago was probably around six years old. If he had anything to say about it, she looked the part, his every cell rejoiced at the memory. He had found her in another park not the one near work, he had been out for a walk when the opportunity landed in his lap, and it was too good to not seize. So, he did, it was a short encounter which has fueled his need even more. He had lured her away easily with the parents distracted with friends and phones, they certainly made it easy. He had managed to have twenty minutes with her before anyone even noticed she was gone. She was *pure*... so *pure*.

This time though, this time he really wanted a little boy to shake things up. A little sweet boy, eager to please. I must keep it interesting, he thought to himself with his sick smile widening, and he needed more time to enjoy them for longer, but that would have to come with better planning. He never liked to rush things, especially in his secret encounters. They were the golden moments that enabled him to endure his daily miserable life with his nagging wife.

Luke

He'd had his eyes on him for weeks, he knew his daily tasks by heart. Around lunchtime he would come over in his grey suit and with his prepacked lunch, probably made by his unknowing loving wife.

Luke knew his home address, where he worked, where he worshipped his forsaken God and even where his children went to school. Luke made it his business to know every little detail about the dirty little fucks. He had an amazing talent for singling out the trash of society.

There he was again, like an old watch, tick, tick, tick... not a second late, eating his sandwich, whilst staring at the kids playing in the park, lusting... It never ceased to amaze Luke how fucking ignorant and obvious these fuckers always were.
    It was not hard to spot the pigs for Luke; years of experience had taught him.

Jason

8 a.m. and Jason was behind his desk with a strong black cup of coffee, his bleak and sad attempt to shake off the tiredness that came with waking up every morning at 4:30 a.m. The note on his table confirmed his suspicions: there were no fingerprints found. Jason leaned back in his chair with his hands locked behind his head, trying to tie together the pieces and understand what happened to Doug Smith, which at this point seemed like the million-dollar question.

Jason caught a glimpse of himself in the window, his wavy brown hair, the dark circles around his eyes made him feel and look older than his mere thirty-two years. Jason never understood the power of his own attraction, those things had never mattered to him. Never being the person wanting to draw attention to himself, he had led a lonely life so far, consumed by work.

The bang from the door shook Jason back into the room and away from his thoughts, at the same time as his partner, Mike stepped into the office. Mike was the opposite of Jason, there was never too much attention and never enough food around. They had been partners for two years and initially Jason had struggled with his loudness and abrupt ways, nothing he could relate to, but two years into their partnership and Jason could not imagine having anybody else better suited to walk next to him or have his back. Mike's loudness could cloud out his thoughts and demons, that was priceless for Jason.

Mike didn't know it but by just being himself he saved Jason every single day.

"What's new?" Mike asked as he plumbed his weight into his chair. His short sandy blond hair framed his large face. And his green eyes looked at him with the hope of new information about the case. Jason knew that he wouldn't like the updates he had for him.

"The man was liked, his wife worshipped the ground he walked on… claiming he was hardworking and loyal, he was into his golfing… I did have a look at the golfing club, it was legit," Jason replied.

Mike leaned back and looked at him with a disturbed expression, and more than that, an annoyance that Jason could relate to. They had spent every day without anything of value coming through their way.

"I don't get it, pretty boy, what are you saying? That he was at the wrong place at the wrong time?" Mike asked, frustrated.

"Of course not! Both you and I know that this is personal, we must keep digging. Sooner or later, something will give, it always does."

Luke

Luke knew it must happen soon, the hunger in the pig's eyes seemed to become like a hollow holes.
 Tonight.
 It will happen tonight.
 Karma has a date with you, Mr. Doug Smith.

Doug Smith

It was his turn to lock up the bank and he didn't mind; it gave him the freedom to enter the office main computer to perv on little children. It was his favorite time indeed, no disturbance from his ever-annoying wife, or his children. Here he could take his time.

He knew this way it would be a long shot to connect it to him, if it were ever to be found out. So far it had been a piece of piss for him, what an easy price to pay to get to be himself with no one to judge him. He smirked to himself. To be able to easily access his dose of medicine, he had to thank the development of the great World Wide Web. It had opened an infinity of opportunities for him and the likes of him, yes indeed it had opened many other things as well, but this was just a miracle for someone like him. He'd read somewhere that around 200 million girls and 100 million boys will be sexually victimized before they reach adulthood, a significant number of these will be lured online, that's when he decided to spend more time online rather than off. Now of course Doug did not agree with the misuse of words such as victimized and lured, those were all perspectives for him.

Two hours later, which had passed by way too fast for Doug, it had started getting dark outside. He closed the office and started walking toward his assigned parking spot. He felt delirious from having had his fix, for him it was better than any drug or drink, it was survival. Walking with an ease and a smile similar to that of a newly self-made billionaire, unknowing of the justice awaiting him inside his car.

Luke

Luke could feel his heart beating fast. He would take himself to where he needed to be to get the job done. He had prepared everything. *Dexter would do well taking a few pointers off me*, he had thought to himself as he was getting prepared. Plastic-covered floors, bath ready to empty his dirty pig life away. The delight of knowing what was coming left Luke feeling alive, adrenaline buzzing through his whole body. Before he knew it, the gun was shoved into the pig's neck, pressing, spreading fear in every cell of this beast. Luke felt glorious.

Two people in one situation, one feeling joy, one in fear. Having heard Smith's favorite quote during the time he had followed him, Luke thought that he was indeed right, it was all about perspective.

Doug's date with fate

The temporary satisfaction had put a stupid grin on his face, as he sat down to drive home to his *loving* family (yet one he would have loved to never see again). He did not realize how close he was to getting his wish granted. Before he drove off, he looked in the back mirror, the last thing he laid his eyes on were the ice-cold blue eyes and a wide sinister smile.

Luke

It only took Luke ten minutes to reach his destination but the work itself took him a good few hours. Hours of joy for Luke and hours of hell for the pig. There were decisions to be made… like where to dump this pig's body? Luke knew it had to be the park, the only place for justice. Luke never cared much for hiding the bodies too much, he wanted them to be found, he wanted their little shit worthless lives to be dissected with nothing, but crumbs left unturned.

Justice

"Oh God…Please don't! I give you anything you want… oh God… oh oh oh Gooooooood!" Doug's face was twisting and turning in agony as he was screaming, to no avail though, as the walls were all soundproof. The sweat and blood on his face had turned into muddy streams, making him look like an old painting of a man being crucified.

The cries of fear and the sobs were clouding the words coming out of the pig's mouth. Luke didn't like that…he liked to savor the moments, the words, the pleas, their fear and desperation. How could he hear the fear with all that whinging? For fuck's sake, fucking asshole ruining this with his fucking tears.

He got himself ready, deep inhale, deep exhale, in… out… faster and faster. He was taking in every second, he could probably smell the fear better and stronger than the rottweiler pulling away in his hand. The rottweiler knew what had to be done, and the piece of steak placed casually on the "pig's" crotch would not leave any room for any mistakes.

1… 2… 3… the rottweiler… the fingers slipping away one by one and very slowly, and then the scream…. Yes, the scream. Luke cracked his neck and with a smirk on his face, he fitted his plastic gloves on his hands, walking across to finish the business. Surrounded by the screams of the pig.

Jason

The day at the office had not been a total waste, the focus was to pinpoint habits and usual places. It was then that the call came in from the bank management. Entering Doug's computer at work they had found "incriminating activities". With one call the door to a whole new Doug had been uncovered. Jason had been the chosen one to break the news to his widow. The reaction had been as expected. Doug's wife initially had been hit by a shock, then anger and denial and lastly fallen to her knees in disbelief. Jason knew the time had come to leave, let the whirlwind settle, although now they had to not only deal with a loss, but also the questions left by her pedophile husband to be answered.

Luke

The feeling of relief from the anger, rage and hate was almost as instant as when his trusted dog set his teeth into Smith. With every scream and cry for help Luke felt more and more alive, as if Smith was surging his blood with life from another realm.

Jason

So, there it was, Doug Smith was a pedophile. Potential killers had in an instant become a wide-open hole with no end. Was it a victim seeking revenge? Were there others involved?

The questions swirled around in Jason's head when Mike walked in with a winning smile on his face giving Jason a minuscule hope that they might have caught a break.

"I just received an anonymous call," he said sitting down. The person claims they regularly visit the park we found Smith in, they confirmed the fact that he would always have his lunch in the park, they also said that during the last two months they have noticed another man showing up at the park at the same time as Smith. I mean don't get me wrong, pretty boy... it might be nothing, just a coincidence or maybe not. I got the guys to sketch and got an image based on the details given."

Luke

It was in the third week that Luke saw an attempt at a drawing looking a bit like him. As much as it intrigued him to know how the police had retrieved this information, he could not help but smirk about this cat and mouse game. Surely, they knew that the victim was a pedophile by now? A dirty pig... they should really thank him.

Here he was providing public service on his own time with his own budget, and this is what he got, honestly this world was fucked beyond any coming back. Oh well, he thought, a few small changes and none of this would matter.

Nightmares

The nightmares, Jason thought would last a lifetime, it already felt like he had suffered them for ten lifetimes. However, they just vanished, as swiftly as they had appeared...poof. Gone. As if by magic... The first night it happened Jason still woke up at 4:30 a.m., as if his body had adjusted itself to the time of terror. It was only after a few minutes that he realized that he had woken up by habit and not by the scream. Three weeks in and Jason had long forgotten about the boy with the knife.

Three months

Three months in and there had not been any murders or violence of the type that Jason and Mike were on the lookouts for. They had spent hours obsessively trying to solve the Smith case, with no luck. Jason could not escape the feeling that someone had done them a favor by taking Smith out, so what if no one was caught? Smith had gone from a victim to a sadistic pedophile rapist who was found dead, in a matter of days.

The world has had bigger losses.

Luke

He had to keep his head down for a few months, firstly to let the situation calm down, secondly and more importantly, Luke needed time to research his next pig.

Dave Samson, "The Priest"

Luke had come across Dave online, in one of the many million chat rooms dedicated to this filth. It was obvious to him that those pedophiles were never going to be the focus of politicians or the police. If they had, it would have never got out of hand like this. He had encountered hundreds and hundreds of sites, chatrooms where these pigs could share images, ideas, conversations and plans without any consequences. He had joined as ten-year-old "Lucas", it took the priest five minutes before he started chatting "Lucas" up, coming across as a friend, whilst all along grooming his next victim... well that's what the priest thought. He was an eager man, little Dave, talking to "Lucas" daily. The methods he was using to get under "ten-year-old" Lucas's skin was awful, but Luke could see how it would and could work on kids, who were trusting, especially towards a priest. Even worse if the kid needed validation and love. These low-lives scums always knew where to find the weakest ones in society and prey on them. There were so many things fucking wrong in our world and society. Luke had never been able to get his head around how you needed to take millions of different tests to drive a car or have hours of training for a job, yet the most important job in the world, being a parent, all you needed to do was just shoot off your load into another person and *voila*, suddenly you are responsible for another being's life and you don't need to know what the fuck you are up to and let alone if you are even suited for it. Humans made Luke despair.

For Luke, Dave was the lowest of the lowest kind of pig, the kind that hides behind his clerk, the dirty kind that preaches to the dumb and blind. He needed a finish worth remembering.

The priest

A priest loved by all, always doing good or wanting to do good, that was the image Dave had managed to dedicate his life to painting. That would have been a great image if it had been true, sadly they were to find out otherwise.

If you asked some of the younger choirboys, they would give you another side to the priest… the dirty priest. A story of betrayal, hate and violence, but this was no worry for Dave Samson, after all he was a man of God, a man who would always be under the wing of his Father.

In his mind the little boys didn't realize that he was there to teach them about love and understanding of the pure gift they have been given. How could this world be so fallen? They just didn't understand the truth…

Jason

Just when he thought that the dream was gone, it had come back. Just as strong, just as clear…

Jason woke up feeling the familiar feeling of fear and hopelessness. When it had finished last time Jason had thought it was a one-off thing, but now it was here again. It almost drove him to insanity last time trying to figure out why it was happening; all the thinking and overthinking had not brought him closer to an answer. He had no idea how he had managed to make it stop, or if it was even in his hands.

He was dreading the thought of not knowing how long it would be with him this time, sometimes knowing what you are in for is worse than not knowing. For the first time he hadn't known what to expect, but this time knowing what the dream involved made it thousand times more unbearable.

The next day

Dave Samson had been found by Ms. Martin, a seventy-five-year-old avid churchgoer. Ms. Martin was always first into the church to attend and help, but this day was different, the church even felt different from the moment she stepped in.

There seemed to be a cold, heavy silence.

As Ms. Martin worked her way slowly through the church, she realized that something had been moved to keep the confession door shut.

Dumbfounded Ms. Martin tried to move the object out of the way and as she moved her feet, she felt the sticky thick blood on the floor. Her scream echoed through the halls and set off the alarms.

Who would do such a dreadful thing to their local priest who was loved by all?

Dave Samson

The confession booth was covered in blood and bits of Dave's body.

As Jason was trying to keep his head awake after the early morning's unpleasant wake-up calls, poor Ms. Martin was sitting on the bench trying to clean off the blood and lumps from her shoe.

Mike was sitting next to her trying to get as much information as he could. Jason doubted it would be much, Ms. Martin was beyond herself, the thought of going home with some of the priest stuck in her shoes somehow did not appeal to her.

The poor woman had walked in for her daily charity work expecting to do her chores and get on with her life, but here she was now stuck with a twist played by fate. Jason would be very surprised if Mike could even get a word out of her that would make sense.

Luke

To get the priest was too easy, and his tears…honestly… one thing Luke wished for every time would be that the pigs would have some self-respect, some dignity… some fucking balls to man up. Even if it would be the only time they did so in their pathetic scum life. But as always, that didn't happen. He had walked into the church and was greeted by the pig. As Luke sat down to assess the situation, the confession room caught his eye. Luke wanted to take care of the pig without too much planning and care, he just wanted to enjoy it fully this time. He felt it in his body and every bone that he wanted this little pig to truly suffer.

Dave Samson

The man had come in early this Wednesday morning, Dave thought to himself. It wasn't often he had visitors this early in the morning unless the few and far between lost souls seeking salvation found him randomly by the hands of his beloved God, Dave thought to himself as he made his way down the rows.

Dave decided not to approach the man, just the mere "Good morning." You get to learn people's ways and habits very easily when you are at the same place every day. Day in and out, week after week, year after year.

Dave knew every member of his church and yet could not place this man. Suddenly he felt a presence by his side. As he turned, he could smell the man's perfume and what seemed to him to be desperation.

"Oh... Good God! I didn't see you there," Dave managed to chuckle nervously, as he was trying to find his balance.

"Can I help you? Would you like to talk?" Dave asked as he tried to step back and create some safe space between himself and the stranger in front of him. Luke looked at the man, up close, in silence. He studied every line, every twitch and movement, desperate to a degree to understand what could drive such a beast but also to memorize all the details of this pig's face before he tore it off. Dave felt the unease creep upon him.

"Oh priest, dear priest..." The man put his hand on Dave's face. Dave knew then that this was not going to be just another normal Wednesday. He could feel the underlying shift, this was going to be a difficult session, he might as well see it through and get rid of this man, who needed some of God's saving light.

"Why don't we go to the booth where you can speak more freely?" Dave tried to ask with a little hope in his voice.

"Yes, why don't we?" Luke met the priest's stare at the same time as he tasted every word. To an untrained eye the priest could be perceived as in control and not bothered at all by Luke's closeness and erratic behavior. But for Luke the slight twitch in the priest's left eye was screaming panic to him. He had got to him. It was beautiful to catch the panic in their eyes, it soothed Luke's soul every time.

Inside the confession room, Luke just felt suffocated, how would anyone in their right mind think this is where you needed to come to cleanse yourself?! Luke shook his head every time life reminded him of humanity. Why we weren't extinct yet by our own hands was beyond Luke.

"How long has it been since your last confession, my child?"

Luke thought about this question and couldn't help but smirk at the charade taking place.

"Now, now, priest, that feels very intrusive… don't you think? Let's start with you… let's build-up the trust… how long has it been since you last confessed, *priest*?" Dave did not know how to answer this question, should he even answer it? After all he was there for people. Dave was the salvation, not this homeless, careless man. How he wished that this man had entered another church and not his, not very fatherly indeed, but he'd rather not deal with this obviously crazy man on such a busy day that he was going to have.

Jason

Although it was easy to see parts of the priest had been splattered on the walls and in the creases of the walls, the priest's body and clothes or any other evidence were nowhere to be seen. What part it was would be hard to determine by looking only, the mess seemed to be all over. Some lumps, blood, and oh yeah, the bloody torn collar thrown onto the floor, half soaking up the blood.

Luke

Okay... so the whole not planning was not his thing Luke decided that last-minute changes had to take place. The church was always going to be dangerous with people walking in and out looking for answers to life, Luke thought to himself.

And this fucking booth is making me very claustrophobic, he thought.

"Dave, would you like to go for a walk with me?"

Dave felt the unease spread more and more through his body; how did he know his name? Where was this man from? He needed to stay here with the man, he could not go with him.

"Who are you?"

"Yes, who am I? Would you like to find out? I know there is someone that would like to meet you. You know him very well, as you made it your business to reach out and get to know him too. His name is Lucas."

The priest didn't connect the name with anyone he would have known to start with, then after a few seconds of silence and his brain darting back and forth trying to place the name, he knew. Suddenly the man in the booth made sense to him, his weirdness and passive-aggressive ways all made sense to Dave now, how in God's name would he get out of this one?

As Dave went to stand up to get a better look at the man, Luke was already on his feet, pulling away from the curtain in front of his face, again too close for any thoughts to go straight. Dave felt the pressure in his stomach from what could only be a gun.

"Walk with me, quietly, do not dare to do anything out of place or I will shoot you and anyone else watching or hearing you!"

From that point on everything spiraled downward fast and out of control for Dave. Even though he knew that it would be a waste calling for his God to save him now, he was going to have a date with the devil.

Eeny, meeny, miny, moe...

As Luke laid out the weapons for his game, the priest was shivering on the floor.

"Why are you doing this? Please talk to me! You don't need to do this! I can help you!"

"Tell me about your oath to *God*, priest! What does it entail?"

Luke was enjoying this part, watching the pig squirm around, pleading his case.

What made them think that they could plead it?

"What do you mean?"

Dave's eyes were full of fear darting from one point to another, aimlessly trying to put together the small pieces of the puzzle that he had in front of him, to make sense of this nightmare.

However, the shock of the events taking place had completely thrown any thinking capacity in Dave.

You always think you know how you would react, or on some level think about how you would overcome situations like this.

However, you will never truly know yourself unless you are in one of these unfortunate sticky situations. And this one was very sticky indeed.

In our reality, we are the main stars and heroes but as the priest would find out, imagination is called imagination for a reason, it rarely happens in real life. Luke paced up and down the table, stroking each knife, his tools of revenge.

The thing that would give his release from this anger, as soon as it sank into this piece of shit's body… and in his head the medley went on: eeny, meeny, miney, mooooe… taking his time choosing… just like the pig did when he took his time to choose his next unknowing victims… just like he did.

Suddenly the perfect finish came to him. He took his finest dagger and walked towards the squealing pig. His grin widened as he knew the pleasures that were to come. Luke's grin froze, what the hell was that? Oh yeah, he'd done it, the fucker had pissed himself. Luke gave him a well-earned kick in his crotch to start the beginning of the end of their very short encounter, however, this was also a matter of perspective.

Wrap up

After a whole day of torture and eventually sending the pig off to his beloved God, Luke rolled up the pig's body in the plastic on the floor and dragged him into the car and back to the church.

The darkness and silence from the graveyard consumed the air. The door was still open, everything still left untouched... oh besides one big matter, the priest was now dead and wrapped up, like a pig in a blanket on the Christmas dinner table.

Once downstairs in the church kitchen, Luke dragged the chopped-up pieces which once made up the priest's body to the mincing machine and started the last part of processing the pig's body. Luke decided to keep the blood of the pig and bits of the minced body to mark his confession room, a perfect ending: to pay with his blood for what he had done.

The rest of the minced meat he decided to take home and feed to his beloved dog.

Oh, and by the way: No, the Lord will not forgive you for your trespasses.

Jason

What even is that? Jason thought to himself as he was standing outside the confession booth trying to gather as much information as possible and at the same time not get any lumps on him or blood. Mike was busy questioning any potential witnesses. Which at this point seemed harder than finding a needle in a haystack. It didn't matter how long a person had been a copper the smell of death was always as overpowering and unbearable, Jason thought to himself, wishing he could cut his nose off to not smell it.

The priest lived in the allocated staff room at the church, as he did not have any family members, it had suited him perfectly when he had accepted this post.
    There were no personal items, in fact, he seemed so impersonal that even having a personal vendetta seemed farfetched. But not that farfetched as he was now spread like chunky peanut butter on the walls of the confession room. But then where was his body?
    The only thing connecting the priest to this scene, besides the splattered blood on the walls, was the actual lack of the priest alive, his few belongings in his room still intact and... oh, again not to forget the blood-stained collar thrown on the ground. It was around day three of the investigations that a few choirboys started coming out with some very insightful information about the victim: David Samson, priest.

Police report:

> <u>Victim</u>: David Samson, 54. Catholic priest at Saint Catherine's Church, Springfield.
> <u>Status</u>: Single.
> Date of Murder: 15.10.20

The normal procedure of Mr. David Samson would be to lock up the church for the day, attend to the congregation, oversee the choirboys and last but not least the daily chores. One by one the different people had been interviewed, and it was when the police started talking to the choirboys that a different side to the priest started displaying itself.

One that would put him on many people's to-do-list.

Mason

Mason was a thirteen-year-old boy. On the outside he looked like any other teenage churchgoing boy, he loved his sport and did very well in school.

In recent months his parents had noticed a change in him, he was a little bit quieter, a little bit more withdrawn. Not knowing any better, they had put down the changes to mood swings and hormones.

It was only after Mason was interviewed for the third time that the truth and the reason for his changes came to light. The priest had started to take Mason in for "one-to-one guidance" a few months back.

Samson the priest had a habit of doing these sorts of meetings so of course Mason suspected nothing unusual when he was called in by the do-gooder priest.

Mason knew that this was something that had happened in the past to some of the other choirboys, so when his time came, he felt special to finally be chosen.

Instantly Mason realized that he didn't like the one to ones, and he wished that he had never been chosen, but he knew he couldn't and wouldn't dare to speak up about it. Was he the only one? Why did he get chosen? He thought he must have done something to deserve this, this must be penance for something… it had to be, surely God would not allow this to happen otherwise?

The priest had overall raped twelve choirboys, counting only the ones that chose to speak up.

Jason

Did Jason think it was strange that within a few months there had been violent killings of pedophiles in the same territory? Sure he did.

Were there obvious connections? Not really, besides the violence - saying that, the level of violence in the second case was hard to determine.

However, one could argue that scraping off pieces of DNA from a confession room would have had a lot of violence incorporated.

The lack of a body, fingerprints or any evidence made it a lot harder to connect them. Did Jason really want to connect them? In his heart, the answer was very clear.

No.

However, in his mind he knew better, he needed to connect them.

Silence

The two murders in the otherwise quiet town of Springfield had stirred up a fear in citizens that before did not exist.

Jason and his department had refused to comment on either case or connect them, to limit the damage. Yet the fear had spread like a wildfire, as it always did.

This ultimately made Luke's job harder, but as always, the dirty greed of the pigs always lured them out, one way or another. All he needed to do was to hold fire, wait and be patient.

The nightmare

Jason's dream had been with him for almost six months after the murder of the priest. But this time it had been almost like a movie, added chapters, people, faces and places. Some he knew and recognized but most he didn't, it was all a blur, a mishmash of his life and what seemed to be someone else's memory of a life. The face of his mother, who had passed away many years ago muddled up, in tears, his father's angry face, whatever he could remember from it, staring at him and the rage, his rage. His father was a bitter man, that was all Jason allowed to remain in his soul about his father.

Jason couldn't remember much of his childhood. Whether that was out of choice or just the way things had panned out he didn't know. What he did know was that the dreams of his father made him feel an unease he had not felt for many years. His childhood felt very brief, sometimes he even wondered if he had had one at all.

His mother had passed away when he was a young boy around four, he thought. Jason found it hard to place time and memories from his childhood, especially after his mother's passing; after that the rest of the memories were almost erased.

His father did not bring any sweet memories to his mind, in fact his father's name brought only things he never wanted to carry in his mind or heart, it always got heavy. Jason had decided long ago to shut that door and never to look back. Whether that decision was made subconsciously or consciously, Jason did not allow a lot of time or thought to be spent on his childhood, not his mum, not on any possible past friends, and especially not his father.

The next real memory he could recall was being seventeen and taking his first volunteer job in the force. Starting as a runner boy to being one of the youngest detectives in Springfield's history. His success rate was unbeaten, but for some reason in the last year, things were getting harder to put in place.

Jason could catch himself lost in time, stuck between reality and dream. He brushed it off as stress and chose to lock that worry away with everything else he had locked away so easily.

Luke

Luke knew in his heart that killing little pigs here and there would not satisfy or even achieve the goal he had. In fact, until now he had not been clear what his end goal would be. The only thing clear was his hatred, which is what had fueled and guided him so far.

However, there had been a shift. He could feel the hunger grow in him for more, to end more of them... ending all of them! The brief encounter with the priest had opened up a door to the unlimited sources of online. After visiting some of the pages, Luke knew where he needed to go, he needed to be a part of the world where these arrangements were made. The platforms used by the pigs, to perv, groom and destroy lives for their own sick needs. He needed to become one of them.

The big World Wide Web - Luke needed to infiltrate the anonymous world, where these pigs could be anyone and more importantly, *HE* could be anyone, without being worried to be seen when following the pigs. There was a clear reason why so many of them were online, and Luke wanted to get as many as possible. So, it would be imperative for him to join their mentality, approach and lifestyle to understand how to easily get them.

He needed to change his approach. He knew that having any expectation that the useless cops would catch them and have any immediate effect on this enormous epidemic, which was swallowing the world in its anonymous embrace, would be like emptying a swimming pool with a cup.

However, he was not the police, he could do better, and he would do better. And he knew where to start.

Richard Sams

Luke had his head down in research in the online world and pigs prowling, when he came across Richard Sams.

Richard was a forty-three-year-old man who was well-known for his charity work, especially the Asian orphanage, which he was in charge of and had started. Richard knew everyone and anyone that was worth knowing. His immediate circle consisted of ex-presidents, lobbyists, A-stars and other pieces of shit, that he had accumulated along the way through the years.

Years of working with pigs had taught Luke that anyone who played with the dogs, well must lie with the dogs at some point. So, what did Richard have to offer that made him so desirable to the top elite? What did he bring to them to make such high and mighty people fall to their knees around him?

Visiting Sams

The Asian Orphanage… really?! Was that the best he could come up with?! Luke couldn't believe the lack of imagination and initiative, standing across the street staring at the sign. He corrected his suit, well, more tried to rip it open with frustration, he hated suits they were so conforming, inhibiting and fucking soulless.

When he reached the reception desk, the blonde receptionist did not even flinch, She carried on looking down, continuing with her typing with a stern face.

"I have an appointment with Sams," Luke said, greeting her with the same lack of respect.

You treat people the same way they treat you, that was one of Luke's truths he always stood by. The direct request made the receptionist look over the rim of her glasses. Her stern look proved what Luke was trying to achieve, he wanted to get a reaction, and he got one. She looked him up and down, and without any further reaction whatsoever, she looked down and carried on typing.

"Do you have an appointment?" she responded without looking up again.

Luke wanted to take her face and slam it against the desk... at least ten times, yeah, ten would suffice. How does a soul become so jaded? he wondered to himself.

"Yes, I do!" Luke said with his head tilted to the side with a forced wide smile. He knew he had to control his temper and tone.

He had had complaints back in the day about his dry and sarcastic tone... some bullshit like that, he had switched off before the person could continue. To be perfectly honest it was a shame that he did not let the person finish now in hindsight, it would have been good to find out all the rest of the adjectives that he was.

"Why don't you do your job and tell him that I want to donate a couple of million?"

Luke said bringing himself back into the room. The receptionist looked up at the mention of the millions, the bitch's face started to change, in fact it started to even smile. Luke could only think of one word in his head: Whore… Two words if he really tried: Fucking whore!

People like this only understood one value and one language, and it was always in currency form. People like this were what the problem was with this world. This world was drowning, and these cunts only had their head up in the money hole, sniffing each other's backsides for it. Luke could feel the rage fill him up and decided to focus back on the big picture, this whore would get hers when the time was right.

"Oh, I'm so sorry," she said, for the first-time stopping typing and she nervously fumbled with her glasses. "Let me contact Mr. Sams right this moment."

"Yes, and advice to you, next time try to show some respect when you are on your work time." Luke nodded at her and walked away to the sofas to wait. The bitch tried to express her apologies but realized they meant nothing; her words fizzled out as Luke walked away.

Two minutes later Richard Sams himself was standing in front of him. Luke could feel his heavy existence even from afar, this man was not into anything out of the goodness of his heart, not as much as he was in it for the size of his greedy needs and self-validation. Somebody was clearly in dire need of his daddy's acknowledgment. Richard put his heavy hands out and his face beamed with a big wide grin.

"Hello, I'm Richard, I don't believe we have met? Please come with me."

Luke responded with a big grin back.

"No! You are right. We have not, I thought you might find a meeting between us beneficial. I am representing a client who would like to help out with your great work with charities, especially the one with the children."

Luke knew that people all have big egos and they all wanted them stroked - when you stroked a big ego like this guy, you were sure to be rewarded, fast. Luke also knew that unlike dealing with the pigs one by one, this would need time, patience and trust and the reward would be the greatest he'd ever achieved.

He could feel it in his soul. Luke needed Richard's trust if this was going to work.

Richard stopped and turned around to look at Luke, it was only a glance, but it lasted long enough for Luke to know that he was being judged. Would this charade be enough for Richard to bite?

Once they were inside Richard's office, more pieces fell into place for Luke. You could tell a lot about a person by the way they carried themselves, the people they surrounded themselves with and the little details they chose to have around them to represent them. At a quick first glance at his office Richard was a lad's lad. Not a picture of a wife, girlfriend or kids around. Instead, there was a big collection of Richard with various ex-presidents, A-list Hollywood stars, and influential partners from his golfing and fishing pictures. Luke could feel the sick taste growing in his mouth. Somewhere deep within he was praying to everything good that maybe he was wrong about all of this, maybe Richard was actually one of the good guys? Just so that he could find a little hope in this world, that not all was bleak, not all was going to hell with humanity.

Who was he kidding? Luke thought to himself as he studied the framed pictures in the room.

"President Waterstone?! Wow! And here, Prince Henry?! Do you go fishing with them often?"

Richard chuckled and said; "Well now and then."

Richard Sams

Two months had passed since Luke had met Richard for the first time. He had managed to convince him that indeed he did have a multi-billionaire that wanted to invest in his good agenda, as surely his agenda could be nothing but good, right?

It had been a hard two months for Luke, who despised people more than anything else. He had managed to make Richard believe that his investor was all about trust. He wanted his spokesperson, Luke, to shadow Richard and learn everything about his charity, as he had narrowed down two charities for his "donation".

This had allowed Luke to get to know Richard extremely well in a very short space of time. It had also forced Luke to take up activities such as golfing, men's clubs and all the things that could be attributed to being a classified asshole in Luke's eyes. But Luke knew why he had to stay focused, and it all was starting to pay off, as he could feel Richard's wall go down - slowly, but it was going.

As Luke's initial judgement had declared, Richard did indeed not have a girlfriend or wife. His passion for helping had started for all the right reasons when he was travelling around the world in his teenage years. His dad's money had helped him along the way, but then the daddy fund dried up. Luckily not too long before Richard could get cozy and truly in with the elite, the spawn of the devil, call them what you like, but they had helped Richard immensely with PR, charities, etc., but all for a price. And this price would become clear to Luke sooner or later, there would always be a price to pay in this world, and eventually, everything and everyone would be for sale. We all have a price tag in this world created by beasts. Richard had invited Luke to the weekend of his dreams, those were the words he had chosen to describe what was going to happen. Luke had no choice but to accept.

Happy Place

Serenity Valley... like something from the Mr. Men books, and to make it even worse they'd named the hotel Serenity Place?! Luke could not understand it when he first moved to Oregon, and it still caused the same reaction every time he heard that name.

When Richard mentioned it the first time Luke felt like he wanted to teleport himself to another planet, how he wished he'd never contacted Richard at times.

He was taking too long and forcing Luke into situations he did not need or want. What if he had chosen an easier way? Anyway, he was here now deeply entwined. Knee-deep in the shit.

Luke had not been told any details, just to be ready for pickup by a limousine by midday, there was no information given about anything else. Only that he would have a weekend out of this world, which would change him forever. This was going to be the tipping point; Luke knew that this weekend would bring him something to get his teeth into. Well, not so much knew as much as he was hoping, wishing, desperately begging the universe. He was coming to the end of his patience with these games, something had to give.

Midday and the limousine were outside waiting, as he had been told. Luckily the driver had already put up the window so there was no need for small talk. He laid back and tried to brace himself for what was to come.

Once he arrived, he was escorted to his room by a very attractive young lady, he felt unease about the potential age of this lady. As she turned to walk out of the room, she put her hand on Luke's arm, it was only a moment, but there was a lingering, eyes meeting that unsettled Luke once more.
"If you need anything... anything, I am here to please..." And there it was, the extra squeeze again finished off with a slight stroke. I mean if she'd tried any harder her underwear would have to come off. Luke knew this weekend would bring the long-awaited reward for his hard work. He highly doubted that he would enjoy the reward, but he knew it would spur him on to continue. At this point, he could feel his hope vanishing day by day, let alone his will to live around Richard.

They had three hours to settle in before the first planned event which was going to be a seven-course dinner with a twist. What this twist would be nobody knew yet. Once Luke was done unpacking, he decided to take a walk around the hotel to familiarize himself with the surroundings, and the assholes invited of course.
Richard had made sure that the whole establishment was rented out for his special weekend, with staff hired from his organization. After walking around for twenty

minutes Luke knew exactly the crowd he was in and safe to say that he was amongst all the sharks.

Three hours passed way too fast for Luke's liking. The dinner was declared, and they were moved into the eating hall. There was food in abundance, served on top of naked women and men. Luke felt the sick rise in the back of his throat.

What the fuck was this? What had he got himself into? They all took their seats. Luke looked around nervously, the noise level increasing with the movements of the chairs and cutlery, drinks being poured, words being spoken louder and louder, fake laughs… all whilst someone's daughter, son or friend was lying there with eyes shut and being served on. They all looked as if they were in their teens. His brain was trying to process everything and everyone, at the same time as he was trying to remind himself that he was supposed to be a part of this world. Nothing could be shown to unnerve him, or maybe the case was he could not show any nerves no matter what he was exposed to. So he took a piece of sushi from the woman's stomach as casually as his mind allowed him and switched off his mind and thoughts, time to play his role.

The dinner was excruciating. Luke did his part well. He participated in boring conversations with the pile of soulless shits on both his sides. Laughed on que and shook his head in false amazement. Once the shitshow was over, Luke thanked anything good before he thought he could say his goodnights and go off to his room.

Suddenly, the room went pitch black, the murmurs rose, and the drama was in full swing, and boy did it have its anticipated effect on the crowd. The murmurs died out one by one, until nothing else but a deadly silence was on top of them.

What the fuck kind of shit show are we going to get now? was all that circled inside Luke's head like a helicopter.

The room stayed black, and nothing happened…

Nothing happened until they all fell into absolute silence, even then a few minutes passed until the real show kicked off.

There was a spotlight in the middle of the room, in the light was a box.

This black and gold box was probably the size of two grown men, tall and 6x6. The dramatic music started blaring out and the sides of the box were pushed down from inside and out stepped ten children. Luke's stomach dropped.

The children were all clearly from Richard's orphanage, wearing his brand on their chests. They walked down between all the tables and started singing a song, the people smiled, pointed, some started writing. Luke was trying to understand and connect the dots, what the actual fuck was going on here? Why the fuck were these kids here so late?

When they had finished the children walked off and a man walked into the spot where the box had been. He stood until the hall had fallen completely silent again, the light was set in a way where you could not really see the man's face.

"Ladies and gentlemen, thank you for joining us for this splendid weekend. We hope you have enjoyed yourselves thus far, we have more in store for you tonight."

Dramatic pause.

"You who have been with us before, we ask you to not spoil the fun for our new participants." (As he said that you could almost hear the dirty smile although you could not see his face.) "Please just make sure that you are in your rooms in thirty minutes at the latest, continue to enjoy this journey."

Why did Luke feel that "enjoying it" would be the last thing he would do? Why did all these people make him want to scratch his eyeballs out? Why was he the only one in there looking out of place?

Luke was sitting restlessly on his lounge chair in his room, doing the exact opposite of lounging. He didn't like not being in control, not knowing what was going to happen. His whole life was based on planning every small detail, on being the one knowing what was planned and was going to happen.

Yet here he was, with the universe pulling the rug from beneath his feet. He could only hope that it would at least bring him closer to the truth.

Just as he laid his head back to try to switch off his thoughts and mind, there was a knock on his door. Luke hesitatingly, yet very quickly, sat up.

"Fuck!" That was Luke's only thought on repeat: "Fuck, fuck, fuck!"

He had a million thoughts in his head: *What do they want? What are they planning?* If he didn't open the door, would that be suspicious? *No, no, I have to open it, this is why I'm here, whatever it is I will deal with it. Let's go...* those were his last thoughts before he decided to switch off his mind from going crazy and overthinking, it was time to act. Outside the door was a man standing with a black suit and tie on and a black mask covering most of his face. In his hand he was holding a silver tray with an envelope in it. Luke reached out for the letter and shut the door.

Dear attendee,

Welcome to our special weekend, we would like to thank you for showing interest and coming to our event. To continue this journey, we require you to remove your clothes and kindly put on the outfits which we have left in your drawer for your convenience and comfort to get the most of your coming experience, you will hopefully find that everything fits perfectly. When you are ready, please find room 616.

Luke looked around and wondered what kind of outfit they were talking about, he opened the drawer, and inside it he found a silk robe with slippers. *For fuck's sake, and now they have to tell me what to wear and where to be? What is wrong with these people? And silk, really?!*

Luke found himself yet again doing what he was told to do, and soon he was standing outside room 616.

For the first time in his life Luke felt bothered... anxious, this was not a feeling he liked or wanted to ever get used to. Anger was his battery charger, and control was his haven, suddenly he felt the lack of both and was completely lost.

Room 616

Luke knocked, but there was no answer. He tried the handle, pushed and it opened. The room was dark, with candles spread everywhere. Unnecessary fire hazards Luke thought to himself, as he carefully walked inside as quietly as he could.

A massage bed in the middle of the room, the fucking cliché was so predictable he thought to himself.

He walked up to the bed and saw a note on it:

We hope you enjoy your treat, lie down and drift away.

All this drama for a massage?! Fuck me, these people were so precious. And clearly Luke's idea of a treat right now would be to fly the fuck away from this shithole leaving all the fucking creeps behind…that was his immediate response in his head but that wouldn't happen, not yet, not until his gut feeling had been proven right.

As Luke laid down, he heard the back door of the room open. He decided to not look up, to not intimidate the person, and for them to not see him looking shaken, disturbed, rattled.

All the true emotions all these pigs should really be feeling, but of course they wouldn't. This was their scene, they knew this by heart, their sick minds craved it. This was where they bred, infested and grew… this was where they felt at home the most. To a fly the web is always chaos, to the spider it's home... Luke felt like a fucking fly, stuck.

Initially he had to use his other senses to understand what he had gotten himself into.

However, the person must have been very light on their feet or just mastered the silent way. No matter how much Luke tried, he could not hear anything that could distinguish or guide him. Suddenly he felt the warmth of the hands-on his back, rubbing and trying to relax him. Luke was even tempted to talk to get a feeling of what the hell was going on, and he hated talking, he really did not want to be pushed that far.

Thirty minutes later and the person had not spoken a word. Maybe this was it? Maybe he had just built something in his head so that he wouldn't feel like he had wasted his time? No... something deep within him kept churning, he felt like this was not it... there was more to this. An hour later Luke was back in his room, more confused than before. As he laid down on the bed to finally process this fucked-up day there was another knock on the door and before he could reply, the door opened. Luke sat up hastily to put the light on but before he reached it, the person or by the sounds of it, persons, let themselves in and put on the dim light.

What the fuck happened to privacy?

Luke straightened himself up on the bed as rapidly as possible, trying to compose himself.

In front of him stood two boys and two girls, they could not be any older than twelve, they were wearing thin robes and they were all were standing with their heads down. Luke's heart sank. How he wished he had been wrong...

Behind them stood a man again with a suit and face mask on. Luke had to restrain himself to not jump on the man and kick his head in, he could feel his breathing getting faster and his rage consuming him. He was right! His gut feeling never failed him.

He was fucking right! However, now was not the time to act… he would get them, get them all when the time was right. Now he just had to play his part in front of this soulless piece of shit.

"We hope you enjoyed your surprise massage, we have delivered your goods for the evening, choose if you like or have them all for the evening, your choice, your fantasy."

Goods?! Fantasy?! Is that what he fucking called these kids? Luke could not even take in the words spoken by this beast, all he could do was to memorize every detail about him, etch it in his memory, his voice, smell… *you will have your day.*

When the man left the room, Luke stared in silence at the four children with their heads down, shaking, not moving, not daring to breathe.

"You can all stay."

The smallest boy started crying silently, Luke's rage was about to explode in his heart. He took a deep breath, trying to figure out how he could help these children now, he knew he could not set them free as that would raise suspicion, and the last thing he wanted to do was to stand out, he wanted to make them all pay and for now he had to lay low.

"Stop crying, all of you go and lay in the bed and sleep, I have no interest in harming you, you are safe with me," Luke said as he was pacing back and forth in rage, trying to calm himself to not scare the kids even further.

The crying boy slowly looked up with his tear-drenched face, in hope, in disbelief at what he was told. The girls walked and the boys followed, and they all huddled into the bed and had their first restful sleep in a very long time. Luke sat down in the chair opposite the bed in the dark in silence, watching, observing, not even blinking to make sure that the four children were safe.

When dawn fell through the window Luke woke the children up and gave them strict instructions to stay silent about what had happened the night before, they were not to speak about it to anyone and just keep their heads down and lastly, he assured them that their misery would be over soon, he would end this. The children were collected by the same man. He tried his bullshit pleasantries, but all Luke could think about was to memorize every detail about this asshole's face, his smell.

Just like his beloved rottweiler would. Like his rottweiler, Luke wanted to jump on him and rip him into pieces, but all good came to those who waited. He watched him as his mouth was moving and making words up that Luke could not register due to his rage.

"Let us know if there is anything we can do to make your stay more pleasant." Luke decided to take advantage of his offer.

"As a matter of fact, I have a request now that you have mentioned it," Luke said

Luke speaking rattled the man who had not previously heard Luke open his mouth, but only momentarily. The masked man composed himself even faster.

"I was wondering if I could keep these kids for the remaining of my stay."

The man's smile behind his mask could be heard.

"We are pleased to hear this; so, you would like to have the same children the remaining nights?" How many kids have they fucking used? How many have been through their system? Luke had 100,000 questions.

"Yes... yes, bring the same... actually..." Luke hesitated but decided to take a chance and start a conversation with him to see what he could get out of this pig.

"I was wondering... maybe it's a bit forward, but do you arrange these sorts of events often and where can I sign up for them? Could you please tell me how it works?"

The man went quiet. His silence was brief... Luke held his breath.

"This is a taster weekend, and yes you can of course sign up for our membership where you can find more details about how and when to proceed with various arranged weekends and even longer getaways. We can arrange anything you like; we are here to serve you and your needs."

The man felt very happy with himself for sharing information with Luke, as he turned to walkout with the children, as if he had solved Luke's every problem with this fucking shit he had spat out.

As if these souls had no value, just a toy for their needs. Luke's restraint became harder to keep in check, he wanted to leave on the spot that morning, but he knew by staying the whole time he could at least keep these four kids safe, at least these four. Just as the man was to close the door the smallest boy who had cried turned his head to Luke as the last begging attempt to breathe and not to suffocate slowly before Luke could stop himself the words came out.

"Hey… hey, wait," Luke said putting his hand up and walking towards the door.
"Yes, sir?"
"I was wondering… maybe this is too much to ask, but I came here for this," Luke said swaying his hand in panic towards the kids. This was not like him but something had come over him and he could not stop the words coming out.
"And I'd rather spend my time with these little ones," he said putting his hand on the boy's shoulder and pulling him back in towards him.
The man's smile could be heard through the mask, yet again.
"This pleases us indeed, of course they can stay with you as long as you please." The children walked back in, each of them with great gratitude yet fears in their eyes. Luke put on his biggest smile and sent the pig on his way.

The following days Luke made sure that the children got to feel like children, although he knew that their fear, pain and worry would not disperse that easily. But what he wanted was for them to feel somewhat normal for a few days, eat well, sleep well, play and watch TV. To not worry or be scared. To just be. It hurt Luke beyond belief watching the kids, now for sure knowing what they had probably been through and would have to go back to.

He explained on the last day as he knelt down to say goodbye, that this would only last a little more time as he would make sure to end their misery soon and set them free. All they had to do was to keep quiet about what had been going on between them and pretend that everything was as it was.

Planning

Luke understood more than ever the importance of acting quickly after having spent a few days seeing and hearing what those children had endured and were still enduring. Now it was time to act. He didn't have a lot of time, every day already wasted was one day too many. He had to get even closer to the inner circle, to find out more and get more names. He decided to carry on playing his part and getting closer to Richard. Richard was going to be the key to unlock the door that Luke needed to open. He needed him on his side for now, and he needed his trust faster.

Jason

Jason's nightmares had gotten stronger in the last few weeks, they had now lasted for a few months, and he thought he was losing the plot. As he was sitting in his office, he caught himself falling into the black darkness of his coffee, feeling as if he was drowning. He just could not understand what was happening to him, he did not like the effect it was having on his work. He had no appetite, no urge to do anything, he felt like a shell held together by the stems, that wanted to explode from fatigue and exhaustion.

Jason's phone went off and brought him back to reality.

It was an internal call: "Jason here."

"Jason, could you please come to my office."

Damn it, it was the big chief. Jason thought to himself, *This can never bode well.*

"Yes sir, of course, I will be right there."

Jason arrived at his office a few minutes later. He could see his boss's stern face and look when he walked in.

"Sit down, Jason."

Shit, this was not going to be a lovely catch-up, was it? Jason sat down on the chair opposite the boss and gave him an effort of a smile.

"Jason, how are you doing?"

Why was he asking him that, had he fucked up at work? Had he done something stupid and could not even remember? Fuck, fuck… *think*, Jason thought to himself. *Think quick what can it be?* His boss brought him back to the conversation and stopped his mind from running even more than it already had.

"Jason! I asked you a question!"

"Good, boss… why?" Jason said with a sad attempt to try to sound happy, and it sounded even worse.

"Well, I think it's clear that you are not doing so good. Have you even looked in the mirror lately it's better you take leave, you look like shit! I don't know what the reason is and it's not my place to ask. But I have to make sure that this place is run as it's supposed to, and no cock-ups due to personal whatever you might have going on. So do us all of a favor, including yourself, go home, do what you need to do to resolve whatever you have going on, sleep, do something."

"Boss, I'm fine…"

"No! You are not and you've been told! Now go and come back in a month!"

Jason knew there was no good in pursuing the conversation, once his boss had made up his mind there was no return, no matter what he said.

Fuck! Jason felt the helplessness take control over him. This job was the only thing keeping him from going insane and spiraling down the hole of this fucking dream, which he could not even make any sense of. His boss went back immediately to his work and put his head down as he signed Jason off by waving him out without even looking up. Jason could feel his world crumbling beneath his feet, he could never sit still…what was he going to do now? What was happening to him? He didn't even recognize himself; he was always on top of everything. Not anymore though.

Luke

Luke was now back to the same usual routine of trying to butter Richard up, and since their weekend it seemed as if Richard felt more comfortable and more at ease. He had invited Luke for another trip. This time it was going to last a week. It was, however, a few weeks away, which bothered Luke as he did not like knowing that those poor kids would have to suffer any longer than they had to. But he knew with the bought time his vengeance would be perfectly planned.

Now that Luke knew what kind of events, they got up to he would make sure to come prepared.

Jason

And so, the downward spiral began. Jason found himself in his dark room on his bed, staring out of the window with his mind going crazy.

Fuck, what's wrong with me? was all he could repeat to himself. Just as Jason thought he would go insane in the echoing silence surrounding him, he received a call from an old friend. Jason explained his situation and agreed with his friend that he should go and visit him, anything would beat sitting alone in his own silence which was slowly killing him.

Jason packed his bags and drove to see his friend. Maybe spending time with an old friend would bring some peace, maybe it was like his boss had said, the stress at work had gotten to him and maybe all he needed was a rest and the nightmares would be over, and he could finally sleep again. He had heard stories about people who had died of sleep deprivation, he had never understood in the past how that could happen. Now he knew exactly how it could happen, he felt it happening to him slowly, day by day.

The week away

To no surprise they had changed location this time, instead of the first shit hole they'd succeeded in choosing another shit hole, Luke thought to himself. It was beyond predictable. Luke was starting to feel the familiar urge to want to end them all, a perfect explosion to end all these fucking asshole politicians and bastards.

"Oh, Good day."

Who the fuck is this then? Luke thought to himself as he was cut short in his sweet thoughts of blowing every asshole here off the face of the planet. He turned around with his biggest, fakest smile on.

"Hi…" Luke said as he slowly turned around. In front of him stood a well-presented lady. Clearly, she had done well for herself or maybe she was born with a silver spoon, who knew, more importantly who gave a fuck. She too could blow up like the rest, as far as Luke cared. He instantly knew he did not want to spend too much time with anyone, he wanted to get to the room and get the kids to him and this time he had a plan.

"I recognize you from our last event." She tried to put her best smile on. Luke could tell she wanted to go somewhere with this shitty conversation… *Come on lady, get it the fuck over with. Spit it out.*

"Oh yeah? I can unfortunately not place you."

Luke tried to not look too much out of place. She flicked her long blonde locks which had been perfectly dressed and her red lips widened even further. Luke thought she carried a huge resemblance to the Joker;

they had the same insane look in their eyes. She put her skinny arm with her red newly- manicured claws out to introduce herself. Luke looked down at her hand a split second too long. He was hoping that his disgust hadn't shown on his face.

"My name is Laura, pleased to meet you...?"

"Oh yeah, sorry, bad manners," Luke said as he reached out too, quickly shaking her hand:

"My name is Luke."

"I suppose Richard has yet again forgotten to mention me. I started the orphanage with him a few years back," Laura said in her low almost milky voice as she tilted her head to the side.

"I just don't like to be in the spotlight... I'm more of shall we say, a silent partner." She continued to smile as she detailed her involvement with Richard. Luke nodded and smiled like a good listener. He also knew that flattery made anyone fall backward as there was nothing like getting your pillows fluffed. Especially someone like Laura, who screamed, *give me attention*. Her long white silk dress couldn't have hugged her slim body closer than it already was. She would practically have to walk around with a sign around her neck spelling the word "Desperate" out to make it more obvious.

"That's a shame, to keep such a beauty hidden away," he said with the most flirtatious look. She blushed. Fuck, why are people so fucking easy and boring to read? Or maybe it was just him being fucking good at reading these assholes. The fact that she was a close partner to Richard made his ears perk up though, there was a potential resource thrown into his lap, and he was not going to waste it.

"Well, let's just say that one of us has to make sure that the goods are delivered."

Was she probing for a reaction? She looked deeply into Luke's eyes, he didn't flinch or change.

"So, you would be the person to speak to about the 'Goods'?" Luke asked without sounding too excited. He could not believe his luck.

Laura, you will be my new best friend! Luke thought to himself as he thanked his lucky stars and smiled a friendly smile at her, which Laura took as a sign of an invitation to carry on. But Luke knew what he'd meant with that comment, he knew exactly what he'd meant.

He left that little meeting achieving what he wanted - Laura had practically thrown her number at him. Luke was going to call her for a "coffee" as she put it. But both knew they were coming to meet each other with very different agendas. However, for now Luke needed to stay present for this week, as he had a master plan in his head.

The first night

The standard shit show is clearly on every time, Luke thought to himself as he was sitting stuck between some sportsperson and another c-list actor, pretending to be interested in whatever crap movie or award they had gotten. It was very easy for him to stay pretty much incognito amongst these huge egos, nobody here seemed to have time for or interest in each other, let alone a face they'd never seen before or recognized. All Luke had to do was to keep feeding their egos and making them even bigger. This time the kids didn't pop out for a show. They had arranged a burlesque show with extremely young-looking girls instead, and instead of serving the food on naked young adults, they had chosen to have the food served by yeah... you guessed it, semi-naked young adults, boys and girls. That's the creativity level, people... Luke needed to get the dinner over with and back to his room without stabbing the eyes out of the idiots sitting next to him or himself, anything would be better than this.

As soon as the dinner was finished Luke rushed back to his room. He sat on the edge of the bed ready for the door knock. As expected, it arrived, he stopped to compose himself before he went to open the door and he was hoping that his plan would work.

"Good evening," Luke said with his most charming smile on as he opened his door. The man with the mask nodded at him and put forward the tray with the envelope. This time Luke was going to play it differently, he smiled back and slowly put his hand out, but this time he pushed the tray back gently.

"I was thinking as you were so kind last time and let me spend my time with, well you know with the Goods, could I please ask you for the same set-up for this week starting from now?"

The man with the mask gently nodded his head and stepped back and walked away. Luke inhaled slowly and breathed out, thanking everything good for the spliff he had smoked beforehand to calm both his nerves and the constant urge to go on a rampage.

The kids showed up at Luke's door about thirty minutes later. As soon as the door shut the kids ran to Luke and embraced him, all sobbing with pain and sadness.

Luke froze, he had never been in this situation before, and he could not think of anything to do or say to make these kids feel any better about their lives. All he could do was to take their hurt to feed his own anger. When the kids had calmed down, they all sat down on the bed and Luke brought them all clothes and games. The kids looked so happy and for a moment, a very brief one, this small moment allowed them to forget about their painful existence.

Luke once again took them through what was going to happen that week. When he'd finished talking, the kids' mouths and eyes were wide and hollow, not quite either understanding or probably just unable to process what they had been told.

Monday to Thursday

The week from Monday to Thursday went by very quickly. They spent their days getting to know each other, having room deliveries and waiting for Thursday night. Luke had been lucky enough to spread joy to four souls who were before they met him in a very dark place. With his existence the kids now had hope. If hope wasn't the best thing you could give to someone then what was?

Finally, Thursday night arrived, the kids were dressed and ready, each of them with a small backpack, some money and a note with an address to get more help.

"You got this! Make sure the moment I open the door, you follow the description I have left for you of how to get out of this resort, there will be someone waiting for you on the other side to help you to get to your safe place. You keep quiet about me, if anyone asks how you got away you say by yourselves, otherwise I will not be able to help the other children here... do you understand me?! The last thing I need to ask of you and although I know it's hard, I know it's not a small thing I am going to ask of you, but I need you all to keep this all a secret. I need a little time, you will know when I am done and then you are free to speak about it, in fact you MUST speak about it! What has happened here has nothing to do with who you are, it was never your fault, never carry the guilt and shame of what others do to you. Promise me!"

The kids looked at each other, petrified, worried and lost but one by one they nodded slowly to Luke's request, looking at each other for reassurance. Luke needed to make this teary goodbye a quick one, it wouldn't serve any of them to sit in this for too long.

"When I open the door, you run as fast as you can, run and don't look back. Not even for each other, trust in each other that you will make the effort to make it. I'll see you guys on the other side when it's all over."

Luke felt their love in their eyes, and he knew that his soul would forever be bonded to these four souls, they had marked each other's hearts and minds. He gave them a silent smile as he quietly opened the back door and let the children out, to be free, to be themselves again. Luke felt his smile widen the further away the kids were getting, in the end there was no sign of them at all. Luke had stood there for half an hour feeling the rare feeling of true joy and happiness. He went inside and made sure he gave himself a couple of slaps and hits. He tripped himself up on some furniture and then laid on his bed and had the best sleep he'd had in a very, very long time.

Friday

Luke made sure he slept in until noon. When he woke up, he thought to himself, *Let the show begin*, as he rolled out of bed. He looked at himself in the mirror and the mess in the room. He leaned over to his left side and picked up the room phone and dialed reception.

"Yes! Now you need to come now! Hurry up!" Luke had made the panicked call to reception a few minutes after he had woken up. He had made sure that he was still in his underwear, looking disheveled and not yet showered.

The story went: the kids had jumped him when he was a tad under the influence, they had beaten him, yes it could have been the drugs he had brought with him, yes how unfortunate... and they had stolen everything, indeed awful, tut tut, he fully agreed.

But worse of all they had *DISAPPEARED*. It was truly entertaining to see Richard, Laura and the man in the mask trying to squirm their way out of a lawsuit. Of course, *I am a fair man*, Luke had thought of himself as he was weighing his options.

"You do understand that our investor might have second thoughts now about investing, considering how easily your Goods got away after abusing your clients? I mean is this how our investments will also disappear? This is utterly shocking."

Luke could feel the shame hovering over the three idiots and he thought to himself that he had to be careful to not overdo his acting. Laura, who had been quiet the whole time, gently cleared her throat and gave Richard a stern look and a gentle nod towards Luke.

Richard panicked and rushed over to sit next to Luke.

"I understand why you might say that... it is absolutely awful what has happened, and I can assure you that it has never happened in the past and it will never happen again. Let's leave this and I will promise that your investor will not be disappointed. I will make sure he gets to meet the man in charge himself who will make him an offer he won't be able to resist. OK?"

He put on his biggest smile and big eyes willing Luke to accept his offered hand.

Luke shook it with a stern look.

"I think I'd rather leave this resort now after this appalling experience. I am sure you can understand and appreciate that?" Luke said staring at Richard accusingly.

"No! Of course! We will have your car ready for you asap," Richard said, walking away, smiling.

Luke shook his head in disbelief when he shut the door. *Holy fuck!* It had worked!

He decided to lie low for a while, partially to plan his next move, partially to make them sweat, hopefully worrying about losing the investment would make them make the next move faster. It proved to be the best way to move forward, as a a few days later Luke received a call from a very eager Richard. He wanted to invite Luke on a trip where he could show him how their investment would make a massive difference and help to reach more people, as the demand for their Goods was so high.

Luke had gladly accepted the offer as he wanted to see how big this thing was, also to see what sick bastards were behind it and lastly to find the best way to end the majority of them. To actually be invited to see how things worked was a perfect step in Luke's journey, he could not have planned it better himself.

The trip

Luke had found it hard to sleep the nights leading up to the trip. Before that he had spent his days and nights trying to locate the children he had set free to see if they were safe and taken care of. To his delight, three of them had gone back home where they were safe. The last one, the little boy, had refused to go anywhere. He had adamantly waited for Luke to come back to see him. When Luke entered his friend's house the boy was sitting at the table. As soon as he saw him, he dropped his spoon and ran into his arms, the sobs seemed never-ending. Luke could only do the one thing that he could do, which was to stand completely still in silence, and let it do its job.

Luke's biggest fear in life was this: emotions, raw and real. He could not think of a more awful situation to be in. It was against everything in his nature, it could not be composed or controlled at its worst. And if it could not be controlled it was not for him. Yet here he was. Fuck you, Richard, and all the sick fuckers like you, fuck you for fucking over kids like this, fuck you for the harm you cause in the name of greed. Luke was running out of fucks. After what seemed an eternity and an ocean of tears, he bent down and gave the boy a strong embrace.

"Why have you not gone home, boy?"

The boy looked down at his feet, which were moving nonstop with Spiderman on them. His cheeks were soaked, his eyes full of hurt, pain and desperation for acceptance and love. It hurt Luke to the core to stare at the damage done by the devil humans.

It always humored him when he heard people or children talking about what they were scared of, and they would name monsters or darkness, when in reality all they were really describing was the absolute lowest of the low of humans. They were the ones to fear.

Luke was brought back by the boy's response. "Because I can't."

"What do you mean you can't?"

"What happened in that place... well... it happens in my house too... in fact... my stepdad and mum were the ones who sent me with that man."

The nonstop underlying whistling sound in Luke's ear had him holding his ear and head out of pain.

"I'm sorry... I'm so sorry, did I upset you? I didn't mean to," the boy said with his tears breaking again.

"No, no it's not you, I just... don't worry I am fine. Okay, do you have anywhere you can go?"

Luke replied, bringing his focus back to the boy.

"I was thinking... I really want to come with you... please?" The boy's eyes looked into his, begging and pleading. Luke's initial reaction was to turn around and run but he knew that he was dealing with a hurt soul. The last thing he wanted to do was to cause another bruise on this boy's soul, he wasn't that person, he refused to be that fucking person.

"Listen, I wish you could but there is too much right now you know... Look, why don't I speak with my friend and you stay here until well until we can sort something out for you?"

The boy's sadness once again took over his whole being. Luke wished he could say why it would never work, but all he could do was give the boy a half-smile. He came to an agreement for the boy to stay with his friend until Luke could sort somewhere for him. Luke's rage which had started as a fire in his heart was now a forest wildfire burning up inside of him, ready to consume and destroy anything and everything. He would make sure that this trip would be the beginning to a long-awaited end, an ending the world would all hear about, the ending that all these sick fucks needed.

Flight

The next day Luke was in front of the private flight part of Springfield-Branson National Airport. He had arrived in good time to make sure that he could be in place to observe and take mental notes.

He wanted to know every detail about this journey, and to make sure he would not miss anything, he had put a bug on his hand luggage. Thirty minutes later Richard arrived with Laura next to him, Richard was dressed in a suit, looking as macho as ever. Luke never knew that he could have self-control around an animal like him. A few steps behind him, Laura was walking, dressed in a suit dress. Luke stood up to greet the bastards with his most charming smile.

"Luke! Great to see you, very excited to take you on this journey and show you how the operations work." Richard said, smiling at him.

"Good morning, Luke!" Laura said with her usual flirtatious voice. Luke could understand why those cheap shots would work with a package wrap like hers, but it did nothing for Luke who saw through and now knew what kind of animals these people were.

"Yes, our investor is very pleased about this step in our relationship, especially after what happened last time, he was not amused. However, your great proposal has got us on your side again," Luke said, analyzing their faces for the slightest change at the mention of the last time they had met.

"Of course! But that's behind us now, right? So, let's focus on what's ahead and what we are going to see next is going to blow his mind and yours!" Richard said all-knowingly.

"Shall we go? Otherwise, we will miss the plane," Laura said as she started walking towards the plane, leading the way.

Once they were seated in the private plane, Richard offered Luke a drink and sat down in front of him.

"So where are we going?" Luke asked, genuinely confused by the secrecy.

Richard looked at him pensively.

"Do you remember in 2012 a UN whistleblower came out and… what was his name again?" Richard asked, looking at Laura who was seated on the other side of the aisle.

"Dr. Mark Leeds," Laura replied with contempt, without looking back from her window view, swirling her drink back and forth. Luke could not remember the name or even think of a time where this name would have ever stood out for any reason.

"Yes him, that's the guy. Well, if you don't know him, let me give you a brief overview. He was a former UN Chief but also a whistleblower, he went on the record claiming that certain famous charity organizations and even one funded by a president, all traffic children and sell them for sex. He also said that major international aid agencies are mainly responsible for the sex trafficking of children in many of the countries they operate in. Especially the one named after a president, spilling the beans that a high number of their employees are pedophiles and guilty of sex trafficking. Leeds was also working for an organization in Yugoslavia, 1996, where he heard of a nightclub, Florida 2000 I think it was called. It was based in Bosnia, where prostitutes were working from the age of fourteen. These girls had according to him been trafficked by this worldwide organisation for their own personal pleasure, from the next-door nation of Moldova."

Richard was trying to add his lowlife charm to his morbid fucking monologue, as he put a grape in his mouth. After throwing a few more grapes into his mouth he carried on:

"Leeds was even a witness when another UN official, K. Molkovac, tried to expose this at the time. This is a lot of information I know, and you are probably thinking why is he telling me all of this, but it will all link, just bear with me. Back to Molkovac, she was first demoted, and then fired. A campaign was launched to shut her up and destroy her credibility, there was even actually a movie in 2010 where her story was turned into a film,

Whistleblower, wasn't it, Laura?"

Laura did not move, in fact she looked as equally bored of Richard's monologue as Luke felt listening to it, hoping that this would lead to something of value. Richard continued:

"They sent an expert investigator into Haiti to find out what had gone on, but when they didn't like what he uncovered, they ended up prosecuting the investigator for fraud! It's the same pattern as Yugoslavia and Molkovac.

So, as you can see there are risks to what we do but the risks are minuscule when you are supported by the giants in the game."

Richard said all this with a big fat grin on his face.

"This my friend is bigger than you and me. I have grown my assets quadruple since I started with this orphanage. The reason why we are on this flight is to go to Haiti for a few days where you can see for yourself where we find our 'goods,' how easy this process is and enjoyable if you know what I mean. But also of course to show you how minuscule the risks are."

Richard sat back in his seat feeling extremely satisfied with his monologue.

Luke kept his calm and looking down into his glass of whiskey, he took a big gulp to win some time to digest everything he had been told, and to also compose himself. This journey would be his toughest one to endure yet, but the information he would gain and the names he would get would make it all worth it. Luke caught Richard's excited eyes when he put his glass down. Luke gave him a big smile and wink.

"Let's do it. I am certain this trip will give me more details about the process to give back to our investor, which would surely cement the investment. Especially if it is everything that you just said to me. I mean, correct me if I am wrong, but by having the big guns on your side, you really do not need to worry about getting caught, as even if you did, the opposition would eventually be shut down?"

Richard gave Luke a big smile and a nod. *He must be feeling so fucking great right now*, Luke thought to himself. *Sick fuck! You will have your day too*, Luke thought to himself, as he repaid his smile with a bigger one. He took another huge gulp of his whiskey to down it all, slammed the glass down and put his head back to sleep.

He was not going to spend any more of his time talking to this asshole.

"Yeah, you nap, boy, you are going to need your rest for what I have in store for you," Richard said chuckling, leaning back and putting his legs up on the seat next to Luke. God, how much Luke hated this prick.

Haiti

The landing woke Luke up. The fact that he had managed to fall asleep around these monsters, knowing where they were going and why was beyond Luke. He felt like a sheep sleeping amongst wolves. Sleep had been his protection many times to separate himself from what he'd had to endure in his younger years, that's how he was used to making the bad things disappear. It's a good thing that some of our habits as kids stay with us, somewhere deeply well-hidden, but always there to pick up. Almost like autopilot, it would kick in and take over.

"Wakey wakey, sleeping beauty," said Laura in smooth voice and with a big smile. Luke gave her an effort of a smile and sat himself up straight as he looked out through the window. As the plane was descending towards Port-au-Prince, Haiti, Luke was taking in the beautiful scenery with the blue sea, and the mountains standing tall and strong. It was almost beautiful enough to momentarily forget about all the dark things that were taking place there, as he looked back at Richard and Laura. And there he was, with two of the people who had brought the darkness.

Luke couldn't understand how he had ended up there, yes, he wanted something big, but maybe he had bitten off more than he could chew?

When they landed, they had a black limousine parked and ready waiting for them. Richard had booked them into Hotel Mont Joli. Thank God, separate rooms, and even better, separate floors.

After they'd checked in, Richard informed Luke that the same night they were going to meet the right of the person, who helped them find the "Goods" for a quick update of how things were going in Haiti.

The day after they would go to the orphanage that kindly helped them with the supply. Luke could see that this was indeed a big-time operation with many, many variables involved.

That evening Luke met Richard in the hotel foyer around 8:30 p.m. and their limousine dropped them off outside the restaurant. When they walked inside Luke could sense that yet again, he would be like a fish out of water.

"Where is Laura tonight?" Luke asked after they'd sat down at their table, trying to sound casual and not intrusive, as he shook his napkin out to put on his lap.

"Oh, she had a meeting with the man himself as he is here, and she also felt a bit under the weather today after the flight, so she thought it would be best to rest for tomorrow."

Luke thought to himself, *Is this it?* The actual guy himself was here! Could this be the opportunity to end Richard now? To end all three of them? Could this be the perfect timing? He knew it could be, but it would not be in his favor to act now. He needed still, he needed to open more doors first, or in fact THE door to the main guy. When he got to that guy, he would end them all. If he did anything to Richard or Laura now that would have been the end of his access to information.

"What a shame, she will be missed, would have been good to spend a little more time with her, but as you said there is more time tomorrow," Luke said with a smile.

"So, what are we doing tonight?" He was hoping to change the conversation from Laura to something else. He didn't feel as if Laura and Richard's relationship was out of choice. In fact, Luke could easily at times pick up a strange vibe between them, almost a bit of competition or even dislike. Richard smiled back.

"Yes, you will have a chance to meet and get to know everyone. Tonight, we're going to eat, and I thought maybe for later we can go and try some of the Goods."

Luke's stomach turned instantly.

"Ok, you don't let a moment pass huh?" He tried to not sound anything else but admiring, although his true feelings were far from that. Richard looked at Luke with a side smile.

"No, my friend, we work hard and play even harder!"

His laughter was echoing in Luke's ear, in every corner of his mind. *You waste of a fucking piece of shit, you absolute lowlife scum, I will make you hurt. I promise you this.*

Luke made sure that whatever he felt on the inside was not replicated in his fake smile as he raised his glass for the cunt opposite him. Whilst Richard was raising his glass to success, Luke was raising his to celebrate Richard's death.

A few drinks later Richard's right hand in Haiti turned up. He was clearly American, he looked very normal, could be someone's grandad or uncle, he was probably both. He sat his heavy body down. He looked

The Boy with the Knife

just like one of the old men you see in mafia movies - leather jacket, oily black hair and a big cigar in his mouth. His small black eyes measured Luke up and down, and with no offer to say hello he took his focus back to Richard and sat down.

"Sorry for being late, last-minute details to deal with." He regretfully put his hand out towards Luke after getting a stern look from Richard.

"Jack Morsey."

Luke gave him a nod and put his hand forward.

"Luke."

Richard took over.

"Jack, this is Luke, he is representing a very important person who is very keen to invest in our business."

"Oh nice, great to hear, so you do actually work sometimes, Rich?" Jack said, laughing loudly, Luke noticed that when the pig laughed his fat shook the table settings around.

In fact, it eventually made the salt fall over. Luke quietly put it up again. He really disliked people who displayed no discipline in their choices, in their everyday life. Filth.

"So, what took so long?" Richard asked.

"Ah! You know same shit, these fucking surgeons think they are gods you know, thinking we are fucking desperate for them. The stupid fucks act as if they don't know that there is someone always behind them starving enough to sell their own mother, anyway he just needed some convincing shall we say," Jack answered, taking a big sip of his drink.

"I'm sorry, surgeons? I am not following," Luke said.

"Oh, don't worry about that it's just a side part of our many projects to make sure that our investors are happy."

"How? What?" Luke asked, genuinely baffled.

"Ok, short story, ready?" Richard said.

Luke nodded.

"Ok, so we have the Goods that you are aware of, but we also help out with organs."

Luke's face must have expressed the shock that he was feeling. The whistling sound in his head and ears came back instantly, so loudly that Luke had to concentrate to be able to hear Richard's information.

"Come on, surely you know how high the ROI is in that business? There are plenty enough poor people desperate enough to willingly give away a part of themselves for a bit of cash that then turns into a huge amount of cash for us." Richard felt very happy with himself.

"And when it comes to the kiddie organs, we just take the ones that are a bit special so to speak, problem solved all around."

"Special?" Luke asked trying to understand what he meant.

"Yeah, you know disabilities, or even if they are too fat or just fucking ugly," Richard said laughing even louder, setting Jack off.

What the fuck had he got himself into? Was there no limit for these sick perverts? Luke could not even lower himself any more than he had. He put his head down and took a bite of his food, anything to keep him busy from talking or expressing his true emotions. Jack stayed with them for another thirty minutes, and then made his excuses and left. For the rest of the dinner Luke's head was in a fog. After dinner Richard took

The Boy with the Knife

him to the office. It was in a building that also had rooms for the children that were staying there. As he started walking towards the entrance, Luke knew he had to come up with something. There was no way he could deal with this shit tonight, he did not want to see a child in pain, tears or fear.

"Shit, Richard I am so sorry, but I think I have to go to the hotel, the food has really messed with my stomach."

"Oh! Come on we are here now, just a quick hello?" Richard said, with his head tilted and jokingly sidestepping towards the entrance. Luke knew there would be no sense trying to reason with him, Richard was tipsy and had his mind set. Luke shook his head and gave him a half-wave to carry on as he stepped into the limousine back to the hotel.

"I'll see you tomorrow, don't take too long tonight, old man, you need your beauty sleep," he said before he shut the car door. Luke was hoping that the last sentence would on some level cause a feeling of urgency and that Richard would not stay long in the building, but he knew better.

That night Luke could not do anything but to stay up and try to digest the monstrous world of these people's lives he had entered. He was facing devils dealing with child abuse and trafficking with an added cherry on top of this pile of shit, dealing body parts. Luke would be lying if he didn't admit how lost, overwhelmed and trapped he felt in all of this. On one hand controlling his rage and anger on a daily basis was extremely tiring and hard, on the other hand he just couldn't wrap his head around these spawns of the devil. How did these cunts sleep, eat or shit with their consciences? How could they go home and face their families? Luke could not get his head around any of this. He just couldn't understand where we went so fucking wrong with humanity. Who decided that all of this was ok? Why were people not raging wars in anger? He knew all the whys, he didn't need to ask the questions. The programming of the simple mind starts very early - to obey and just fucking be able to survive by giving the bare minimum of the crumbs on the table to the normal people meant that they would never have time or energy to question or fight. The game was rigged on a very high level, he knew this. How would he take on this fight all by himself?

Luke decided that starting somewhere, anywhere, even if it meant a small place in this big mess, he would dent these fuckers as much as he could. He would do his part, he refused to be a person just like everyone else, who sat by and watched the world burn. He simply refused.

Luke decided that he wanted to spend more time with Jack on this trip to learn more about how and where they found their victims.

Second day

The following morning both Luke and Richard looked like shit but both for various reasons. Laura was fresh as a fucking daisy. Luke could see who the brain was in their world, safe to say that the showmanship was left to Richard for a reason.

"Morning," Luke said, short but he made sure he had half a smile on to play away from the hatred that was eating him up from the inside.

"Good morning, Luke. How did you sleep? Good?" Laura asked.

"Yeah, sure, good. How about you, Rich? I take it not too good as you are down here with sunglasses on?" Luke asked.

"Mhhm…" That was about what Richard could muster up the energy for. Laura gave Richard a judgmental look up and down and quickly moved her attention to Luke, whilst rolling her eyes.

"Well, I am certainly glad that at least one of you has the decency to take this trip seriously, I am sorry for how Richard has chosen to show up today," Laura said, clearly bitter and so over his shit.

Luke could probably relate to her pain; he was over Richard just a few months in let alone if he had to spend years with the asshole. But that was where everything ended when it came to relating to any of these assholes for Luke.

"Oh, it's okay Laura, please could you get me up to speed about today? What is the plan?"

"Right, you managed to meet Jack briefly yesterday. So, I thought we could go to the office, and you could get a glimpse of how things work and how we are set up," Laura said.

Luke nodded and smiled, "Sure."

After breakfast they made their way to the office.

The office was a six-floor building with ten rooms on each floor. In each room, they could facilitate four kids, so at any time they could get in 240 kids.

They had managed to produce a very nice-looking facade, just like themselves, so that from the outside they represented what would look like a very successful caring organization, all of it to hide the ugly truth, and it had worked for many years.

As they were being toured around, Jack was sharing what he thought was useful for Luke to know.

"As you can see, we make sure that the kids have a good set-up, you know what they get here is so much better than their own set-up where they are from.

During the period when they are here, they get evaluated for illnesses, health etc. After that they get divided into value, just like stock," Jack said with laughter at his own joke. Luke thanked the god of weed once again for keeping him absolutely neutral and numb enough not to react to this devil.

"We divide them into three sectors depending on costs: the finer Goods get sent to the countries and people who have paid good money for their goods, the ones who are healthy enough but too old or less wanted we use for the 'health' department, if they are old and not too healthy we use them to simply deal with the 'supply of merchants' in Haiti and smuggling to other countries, of course they never travel alone on these trips. We always send someone who makes sure they stick to the rules, otherwise we simply finish them on the spot if they prove to be too problematic and not worth their value.

That's more or less the business side, now touching upon revenue.
As you yourself know, people in these fields pay a lot for their goods, what they don't realize
is how cheaply we get them. The good thing with these poor countries are that 100 dollars gets them far and costs us very little, whilst we sell them for much, much more than that."
He looked so fucking pleased with himself, Luke really wanted to grab a baseball bat and separate his head from his body.
"So, 240 kids huh? How often do you turn it around?" Luke asked as casually as he could.
"Every other month more or less, we try to keep it to that but of course this depends on doctors available to do the checks, on orphanages and parents, family members desperate enough to want to hand the Goods to us for a small exchange of money shall we say," Jack replied.
"Orphanages?" Luke asked.
"Oh fuck yes! There is a huge market there, white people don't realize that a lot of their brown and black babies have been put in the orphanages by relatives who want to make some extra cash. Who cares, they probably have another ten, right?!" Jack's fat moved around once again as he laughed at his own joke.

Luke's thoughts for some reason went to his Pitbull and how much he would have enjoyed this asshole, if only he could have had the possibility to put his teeth into him. If only...

"Where and how do you deal with the money? I mean there must be a lot of cash being moved around. I am only asking as I am sure that would be a worry for my investor as he would not want anything connected to him," Luke asked, trying to look around as if he was inspired and not at all analyzing how he could come in on his own and free the kids and blow the shit up.

Jack chuckled again: "With all due respect to your investor, we have people involved in this from ex-presidents and very high and influential people who are still living their best life and being praised as heroes, and no one knows what actually goes on.

When you have propaganda TV and internet in every household, it's very easy to make people think what you want them to think. Especially if you own most of the channels, but to answer your question directly we have a way to fly them in and divide them into the accounts set up in the USA through charities etc. See it this way, humans have been a trade since the beginning of time, it just shapeshifts."

"Interesting." That was about all Luke could get out for now.

When they got back to the hotel, Laura informed Luke that if he would like to see how it worked with the "process", they were going to have a procedure that night. Luke nodded, although nobody actually explained what it was exactly that he was going to see, only to be ready and that he would be picked up with the limousine and meet Jack there.

Process

Luke made his way over to the office at the time he had been given. He walked inside and found Jack in there waiting for him. He started with his jibber- jabber again and Luke decided to take the role of random chuckles and easy questions here and there all whilst his head was trying to gather every detail.

They took the elevator to the bottom floor. Jack opened a hidden door and started walking down a dark alley. Luke clocked that there were no cameras in that part, and a mental note was taken.

Jack put his finger up for the print to open the metallic door, and once he pushed it open Luke could see inside where they had set up three operation tables. At each table there was a doctor all ready and masked up for the surgeries, there were nurses on the side and a man with a machine gun, ready to finish whoever tried to run. Jack pointed to a corner for Luke to stand by and observe, then he flicked his finger at one of the guys with the gun and pointed at another door that was shut. Jack whistled as he pointed to the door to be opened, the man nodded and went to open the door.

When the door opened, what looked like three teenagers walked in with their operation clothes on. Luke could not believe what the fuck was taking place in front of him. He had to detach, he had to detach, he had to fucking detach. His own spit felt like razors going down his throat, the room seemed to close down on him. The words we're echoing in his head, and he went there, his safe place, where he sat back, observed and shut emotions out.

One of the youngsters started wetting himself, he could not hold his tears back as he was walking across to the operating table. The two girls had clearly taken themselves to their safe place in their heads, just like Luke. They were not showing any emotions.

They were just empty shells being moved around; they had surrendered.

They were laid down on the beds, the boys' sobs grew louder and louder, gasmasks went over their noses, and they were gone into a deep sleep, as the surgeons started making their moves.

It almost looked like a synchronized dance, as if they had practiced for years together. Luke felt his heartbeat so fast he thought he was going to have a heart attack. As he went to follow his instinct and jump up and take them all on, Jack turned to him and said, "Let's go."

His words shook Luke back into his reality, and before he turned to walk back with Jack, he grabbed the surgical blade which had been left on the table next to him, slid it up under his sleeve and started walking.

He had to think fast, and he needed to act even faster. Once the big metallic door had shut behind them, Luke grabbed Jack by his hair and pulled him back, he put the knife by his ear and slit his throat. It all happened in a blink of an eye, Jack had no time to blink, let alone to react or think. He dragged his body to the door and used Jack's thumb to open the door, he decided to cut his thumb off in case he needed to enter again. Jack did not need any of his thumbs anymore as it turned out. Luke knew he was very limited in time. He went to the kitchen and took out the butcher's axe, a few bin bags and went back. Luke had never chopped so fast in his life, he cut Jack the cunt into smaller pieces and put him in the bags, and in the dark, he changed his clothes into the new ones he had brought in his backpack which now was full up with tiny Jack parts.

He could hear the people behind the door wrapping up their surgeries. Luke needed to tidy up the scene, yes it was dark and no cameras, but the smell would make it suspicious. He had brought with him chlorine and cloths and gloves and started cleaning like a madman. When you have a habit of ending bastard lives, you know exactly what you need to bring as back-up, almost like a mother who travels with her baby bag, ready to serve.

Five minutes later he made his way casually to the security room to see if he could see anything that had been filmed. Luckily, whether they were understaffed that night or whether this was how they ran their business, none of the cameras worked.

Luke walked out to the limousine calmly with Jack chopped up in his bag. The short bastard was very heavy to carry.

"Could you please take me to the most beautiful sea spot you have?" Luke asked.

"Of course, sir," the driver said and drove off.

At 1:30 a.m. Luke waved the limousine off and said he wanted to go somewhere by himself and that there was no need for him to hang around. He walked off on the bridge and made sure no one was around as he parted ways with what was left of Jack's fat cunt's body.

Had he thought anything through? No.
Did he know what he had started? No.
Did he care? No.

All he knew was that he could not take it anymore, he needed to have a release and Jack had it coming anyway, again he had done the world a favor.

Breakfast

The following day they were flying home. Down in the hotel foyer he could see Laura pace up and down, as she kept dialing nonstop on her phone with no luck.

"Damn it! Why does this man never answer his phone when I call him?" Laura said, frustrated.

"Who, Richard?" Luke asked, pretending he had no idea.

"No, not Richard. I can't get hold of Jack. Did you not go to see him last night?"

"Well, I went as you said, he was not by the entrance, so I walked in, and he was there. He took me to the surgery room where we stayed for a while, then we said our goodbyes and I went to the seaside to contact our investor and talk in peace where no one could hear us, and here I am now. Why? Does he normally disappear? Has this happened in the past?"

Luke tried to sound as helpful as possible and at the same time adopt the distressed look on Laura's face.

Laura looked down at her phone as she was tapping it looking for answers: "Well, he can be hard to get hold of sometimes, I'm sure he is fine. Where is Richard? If he does not come down soon, we'll miss the flight!" Laura put her mobile phone back in her handbag. Richard was down a few minutes later.

After being told by Laura about Jack not answering, Richard looked at Luke.

"Did you not meet him last night?"

"Yes, he did, Richard," said Laura, "and then they parted ways and Luke went in the limousine after the encounter. Can you think if he was meant to meet someone else last night or this morning?"

"No, not that I know of, but I am not his fucking babysitter Laura, how the fuck would I know where he is?" Richard snapped back.

The tone between these two had not passed Luke by, this relationship was as sick as the rest of the set-up.

"Great! We have to go now, hopefully we can get hold of him later," Laura said as she grabbed her hand luggage and started walking.

Luke had felt a little bit of release when he cut the pig's throat open, but he had plans to make, his head was spinning around trying to process everyone he had met and everything he had seen and heard.

When they landed, Luke made sure that they walked away feeling how grateful Luke had been for this opportunity. He managed also to let them know how very interested his investor was, especially after hearing all about the other side businesses they had and other venues for profit.

Richard smiled at hearing this; Laura was still trying to figure out why Jack was not answering.

People disappear, it happens. It seemed to happen an awful lot to kids around them, and heck, sometimes the tables turn.

Jason

Jason had come back from his trip, still not feeling any better. His friend had told him that he had spent his time there mostly sleeping, if this was the case why did he feel so tired?

He was really losing a grip on his life, maybe he had a terminal illness? Could it be Alzheimer's? He just didn't know anymore. Something was not right.

Maybe he needed to go and see someone, how would that affect his work? Would they let him come back if he was insane? He had worked too fucking hard to lose it all, and over what? A fucking dream that was driving him insane.

Weeks later

Luke had made sure to stay in constant contact with both Laura and Richard, just to keep a tab on where their heads were with regards to Jack. Turns out everybody is replaceable, more so in their artificial world, they had counted their losses and hired a new "Jack". After all, the role he played came with a lot of risks, dealing with the people he'd dealt with would always come with certain dangers of being kidnapped or killed. Maybe he had been offered a better offer with better money? That could lure anyone away if they were not strong enough. And with that, Jack was a closed chapter in their lives.

It was also decided that now the "Investor" had seen the other part of the establishment, he would like to see who the person was in charge and running things in the USA. Could this be arranged please so that he could invest as he was so eager? Of course, it could, Richard had assured Luke, it was music to his ears, but of course it could not happen overnight as he was a busy man, and he would have to be patient and a meeting would be set up when the time was right.

Of course, Luke had smilingly accepted and understood.

Toby

Luke decided to take a few weeks off to take care of the boy who had stayed with his friend. He realized that there would never be an easy way to make the boy legal and have him leading a normal life without going through the shitty social service system and being fostered a million times and probably becoming more fucking damaged because of it. He could not do that to the boy, there was always another way. And he found his. He decided to use his contacts and fake a birth certificate and social security number. Once he had the papers, he went to his friend's house to break the news to the boy he had chosen to call Toby. He told Toby to pack his little bag and come with him. He took him to a diner around the corner and bought him a feast of a meal. Burger, fries, milkshake and to finish it off, some pancakes. Toby's grin had been glued on his face from the moment Luke had opened the door until he had finished his monster of a meal.

The Boy with the Knife

As he leaned back to digest his food, Luke leaned forward and said, "Was that good, Toby?"

The boy raised one eyebrow sat up and looked around him to see who Luke was talking to.

"Who are you talking to?" the boy asked, confused.

"You," replied Luke and handed him the papers.

The boy took them and started reading. A few moments later he looked up at Luke with tears washing the remains of ketchup and milkshake off his face.

"Are you? Have you…?" The boy's sobs were so loud that people turned their heads in the diner to see what this man was doing that was making the boy so shaken up.

Luke put his hand on Toby's hand and just nodded. "You are coming home, Toby."

Toby shrieked out of happiness and threw his arms around Luke's neck.

He had finally found his happy place, and Luke knew that Toby would never ever get abused again, not if he could help it. Luke felt the warmth of the boy's tears and desperation, his happiness was feeding Luke's soul.

The transformation of being responsible for another being had come quite naturally to Luke, more naturally than he could have ever imagined. Then again Toby was such an easy kid to be around - having lived such a horrific life, he was grateful for every little thing given to him, whether opportunities or the slightest bit of affection. How could adults fuck up something that was so easy?

Within a few days Toby had been enrolled into a school and his normal life had started - as far as the rest of the world was told, Luke was Toby's dad. This of course meant that Luke had to move from the neighborhood he was in to keep nosy fucking neighbors out of his business. But not only for that, he now needed to live in a safer place as he had Toby to think about. Their agreement was simple. Toby was to never speak about how he had met Luke.

One day he would sit and tell him everything. But not now, now the boy had to breathe and feel what every child had the right to, to feel safety, happiness and growth in a supportive and loving environment.

Luke wished he could save each and every child he had encountered in his journey since meeting these fuckers, but he was only one person. He would do his utmost to do maximum damage, whatever he had in his power he would make sure he'd use.

Jason

Jason had completely given in to what seemed like his breakdown. With the job cutting him off and not giving him a reason to carry on, he decided to do what made sense. He went out and bought bottles of vodka and whiskey and locked himself up. He decided to drink his way out of this fucking insanity and hopefully make it to the other side alive and in a better place, isn't that what people say anyway when you go through shitty periods? To not care, to not take things so seriously. To just have fun. *Well, let's just have some fucking fun,* Jason thought to himself as he poured himself another glass of vodka.

Laura

What had happened to Jack? The Jack she knew would never ever just disappear! He loved the money way too much to risk anything. They had been working together for decades. So why now? Luke had been the last person to see him, the limousine driver had confirmed that Luke had walked out alone, and the doctors had seen them both leave together, yet Jack had vanished into thin air.

Laura had from the start felt unease around Luke, she didn't know why. She had tried to work Luke out from the start and could not put her finger on it, but something was off. The way the kids had just got away and now Jack had vanished. She had tried to get info about Luke but there was nothing to dig up. Nothing that stood out, in fact, he had led a life outside social media, and was very, very private. Maybe that was what made Laura feel such an unease, his need and want to stay so private. Maybe she was reading too much into it considering his private fun-time activities, was it really that strange that he wanted to be private?

Probably not, Laura thought to herself as she tried to move on from her suspicions and go with Richard's take on everything. Which was that Jack had got involved with the wrong crowd and had probably been taken care of. Laura got up to get ready for the day, shaking Luke and everything else off her. But she knew that the nagging feeling inside her was there for a reason, for now she would just have to wait and see.

Luke

Luke spent the following week with Richard, where he was taken through how the finances were distributed and costs for their business and how much the investor could expect in yearly returns for his contribution.

Of course, Luke made sure that their business could only be finalized once he had met all the important players in the company to make sure that his investor could rest assured that everybody was trustworthy, being that he was of such importance.

Richard reassured him that he would get to meet the man in charge at the Christmas party happening at Congress Plaza Hotel, which of course he was invited to with the investor as well.

Congress Plaza Hotel, Luke mumbled the name over and over in his head. He had some planning and arranging to do.

Congress Plaza Hotel

Luke now only had a few weeks to gather as much info as possible about the venue and enter it before the Christmas party to arrange everything he needed.

It was always so much easier to enter a big hotel. He dug out his maintenance outfit which he had bought many years ago in the name of research and it had never failed him. He grabbed his toolbox and got into his white van with his fake company name on it.

To enter the hotel had been easy as always: "Yes, I have been called in for plumbing work. Yes, here is my business card. What? No, it's urgent, ma'am. You need to let me go through before there is water damage."

And voila, he was in.

In the time and days of coronavirus, he just needed to follow the rest of the sheep and put a mask on, and nobody would even see his face.

He clocked the laundry room and managed to steal outfits to enter as a cleaner and a name badge. What Luke needed was a map of the building, access to rooms and floors where the security cameras were, and he would have everything set up for the party.

In the following weeks, Luke entered the hotel on a daily basis, stealing more work costumes to enter various departments and rooms to gather info for this party. The party of all parties, it would be one for the books, Luke thought to himself.

The invite

Ten days before the party Luke received a personal delivery. When he opened the door, there stood the man with the suit, mask, and a tray.

Luke stretched out his neck to look out in the hallway to see if any of his neighbors had seen this freak standing there, and to his luck, no one was around. Luke quickly took the envelope and shut the door before anything could be exchanged more than necessary, which could prolong keeping that freak outside his door.

He opened the golden envelope:

Dear Luke,

Please accept this invitation to our yearly gathering to celebrate Christmas together.
This year we will gather at Congress Plaza Hotel, as always you can expect a top show and service. The hotel will be to OUR disposal only during these days, as your privacy is of utmost importance for The Asian Orphanage. We look forward to seeing you all, to show gratitude for your support, which is continuously making us stronger and stronger.

<u>Date</u>: *12th of December until 15th of December.* <u>Attire</u>: *White Tie Dress Code*

Oh, how very lovely!

Luke could feel his butterflies and his joy rise again, finally this was going to an end. Finally, he could deliver his truth, He simply could not wait, he felt like a little child on Christmas Eve, well not that he'd ever had one that he could compare to how to feel, but what he imagined they must feel like. Luke made sure that Toby was looked after and that he had enough in the fridge for him to be away to finish what needed to be done.

The night before he had made sure that his tools had been hidden and put in various places in the hotel. Him being able to access the hotel for info had helped massively, as he had seen the layout for basically everything. He knew what number Richard was going to be in and what number Laura was going to be in.

Laura was going to get her own medicine; she was going to be sent the same way she had sent so many young girls and boys.

He kissed Toby goodbye, reassuring him that he would be back for him. He was not so sure about it himself, but he knew he would do his best.

The beginning of the end

Luke visited the hotel the day before and on the same day to make sure that every tool he had hidden would be in place. His stolen outfits from the kitchen and maintenance had come in handy to access each and one of the areas that would be used.

Once his check on the day was done, he walked out in his maintenance clothes and cap to later return as Luke, the very eager investor.

He was checked into his hotel room. Had he not been in and out what felt like a million times already, he would have been more impressed by the venue, and the efforts made into making this party take place.

He unpacked his bags and patiently waited for the guy with the envelope.

The door knock came but this time instead of the man with the mask and suit he had in front of him a very young girl wearing the classic playboy outfit, ears and tail all attached. Luke looked her up and down. The poor girl was about to pass out from not being able to breathe, probably because she was so fucking nervous. Luke smiled at her:

"You and me both, just focus on your breath, all of this will end one day."

The girl didn't know if she should smile or cry.
Luke took the envelope and shut the door behind him.

Welcome and thank you for joining us.
We are delighted that you have chosen to spend your time with us, we also hope that it will all be worth your time.
Please join us for dinner at 8:00 p.m.

Dinner

Luke made his way down for dinner at 7.55 p.m. He stood in a corner as he normally would and started taking mental notes of the bastards that had joined this party. He could see royals from various countries as well, that should have shocked him more he guessed, at this point, he felt as if he had seen it all. Richard seemed to be very close to the royals as well, the way they were standing and talking. Luke could tell that they had history, and now Laura had walked over to them, looking as sneaky and fake as always… Oh shit, she had clocked Luke watching them. She locked eyes with Luke from across the room. Luke felt like a rabbit caught in the headlights and he nodded towards her to crack the ice wall building up between them. Laura raised her glass and gave him a short nod, and before she turned back to the prince and Richard, she made sure that Luke was aware that he was being watched, by locking eyes with him again. Luke gave a nod back and a half-smile:

Don't you worry bitch, soon there won't be anything to watch you fucking whore.

Luke endured what he was hoping was his last meal surrounded by assholes. It was a seven-course dinner again served on and by half-naked youngsters, it was hard to decide whether most of these fat old men were drooling because they were hungry for food or because of the people serving them, either way just by being around them Luke felt sick. God, how he wanted this to be over. Especially as Laura, the bloodhound seemed to have picked something up. Richard was busy as ever being a douche bag; he would never sniff anything unless it was under thirteen Luke guessed.

As he prepared to leave for the evening, he could see Richard making his way over to him.

"Hey Luke, how is everything? You enjoyed yourself so far?"

"Yeah, you've done it again," Luke said, keeping up the charade.

"Yeah, I mean this part really has nothing to do with me, all this fancy shit is Laura's doing."

"Right, well then, she has done a great job. I will have to make sure she knows," Luke said with a wide smile.

"So, I have managed to arrange a meeting with the top man himself, he was also a bit curious about yourself and your investor, you will meet him tomorrow night for dinner around 8.00 p.m. It will be in room 616, just make sure to be in time, he doesn't like people to be late."

"Sounds great, I have looked forward to meeting the man behind this brilliantly, clever and might I say ballsy business."

Richard lifted his glass to give Luke a cheer to his statement as he started walking away shouting out hellos to people whom he was passing.

Luke stood still and watched him walk away, whilst his mind was running around in circles, in excitement and hunger for their blood. He was going to finally see the cunt in person.

He made sure that no one could disturb him tonight, he needed his full sleep. He hung up the 'do not disturb' sign on his door.

He wanted to be alert, awake for each moment. He also knew that when he finished the cunt tomorrow, he had to make sure to take care of Laura, otherwise she would cause him problems. And he just didn't have time to deal with all of her dramas, in the midst of everything else.

When Luke finished his meditation and stood up, he caught a glimpse of his muscular toned body, and he gave his own reflection a huge smile as he pulled down the sleep mask before he entered his bedroom.

Tomorrow.

Tomorrow. Tomorrow. Tomorrow. Tomorrow.

He slept like a newborn baby falling asleep in his mother's bosom the whole night, whilst dreaming about ripping the cunt's ears off with his bare hands.

The day of the night

Luke woke up well rested for what the day had in store and after an hour of exercising and meditation he made his way to breakfast. As he was eyeing up what to have, he felt a hand behind his back, giving him a squeeze to get his attention. Luke hated to be touched, he could never understand why people thought that was okay to assume that people wanted to be touched. He pulled himself together so that the person would not feel alarmed due to his reaction. As he turned around to see who was demanding his attention, he smoothly maneuvered his body backward, and away from the hand.

"Hello Luke." Of course, it had to be her, who else would want to make his life more difficult now if not this cunt?

"Oh, hi Laura, didn't see you there," Luke said with his friendliest smile.

"No, I guess I sneaked up on you, how are you? I was thinking we've not had much time to talk, would you like to have breakfast with me please?"

Luke could feel the familiar feeling of being cornered.

It takes a lot to play a player Laura, you should know this, Luke thought to himself. *Bring it on, bitch.*

"Yes, sounds like a brilliant idea, I was thinking the same, I am glad you've asked me."

Laura gave him a smile as wide and as fake as his own. Luke thought it was a shame she was a fucking monster, they could have worked well together, but now they had met this way, and it could only end in one way. And one way only.

"Well why don't we get our plates ready and meet over at that table?"

Luke looked across to where Laura had pointed, there was a table with two seats a bit further off from the other tables.

Interesting choice, Laura. Let's have it out, shall we?

A few minutes later both had sat down with their plates in front of them. Luke's quick glance at her plate confirmed what he knew, she was not there to eat breakfast she was down there to give a message to him, and boy he was so ready for it.

He was going to play it cool and let his silence make her uncomfortable, after all she was the one calling this breakfast meeting. *So spill your beans, woman. If you think I'm going to help you in putting me on the cross you can think again.*

"So how have you found your time with us?" Laura asked without looking up from her two slices of watermelon.

"Yeah, it has been very enlightening, and I must say amazing to watch someone having the cojones to go this big in a, shall we say, field that you guys have gone. This is the sort of thing that really interests us with our investments. We like to put our money in ideas that stand out and make a difference."

Luke saying all of that shocked himself... for not choking on the shit he was spewing out to please this devil of a woman.

"Yeah? That's good to hear," she said with a half-smile. "I was wondering when the investment would actually come through, but then Richard mentioned to me that you are going to see our main boss tonight?"

"That's the plan!" Luke said as he sipped his coffee.

"Well, about that..." Laura said, putting her hand on Luke's. Luke didn't, despite every fiber in his body telling him otherwise, pull his hand away. He kept it still and slowly raised his eyes to meet her green, swamp-like eyes, which were like dirty water swirling around, drowning everyone and anything. Nothing about this woman was attractive. No matter how much she tried to hide behind all the expensive brands and makeup, the poisonous smell was too strong.

"Yes? What about that?" Luke asked, keeping eye contact.

"Well, the big guy, he can be a little bit abrupt, are you sure you would like to meet him alone? I'm thinking maybe it would be good if Richard, or even me was in there with you?"

Luke sat back on his chair, he looked at their hands on top of each other, he put his other hand on top of Laura's, and made sure that he kept her eye contact for a good ten seconds as he waited for his pastry to be finished and swallowed before he gently gave her a squeeze and a smile.

"Laura... you do not need to worry, I will be fine. At the end of the day we are meeting as there is a mutual interest in money, profit and getting our businesses bigger, what would there be to be short about? We also need someone to keep a track on our Richard whilst I am in a meeting. How about if you feel worried about how it will go, I can come and see you in your room after to give you the update on how it went?" Laura did not expect that reply and now she was cornered. Luke enjoyed seeing her desperately trying to counter with anything to get her way, it was clear that this little princess did not like hearing a no, or not having it her way.

She looked at Luke with sore disappointment which she was trying hard to conceal with her fake smile.

"Yes, that would be great, as you can understand this orphanage has been my baby since we started it, and I would love for it to grow and have the best potential we can offer for everyone involved." She said as she gave Luke's hand a gentle squeeze.

"Of course, I completely understand," Luke reassured her as he sat back to finish his coffee.

I totally understand, you fucking control freak.

Luke wondered if he could sense some panic in Laura, probably felt as if control was slipping her by. Richard was out of control and Luke himself had landed into her life from nowhere, from what she must believe. Jack disappears, kids disappear, yeah you couldn't blame her really for putting two and two together. But surely, she must have known that all of this would come to an end at some point.

Surely, she must know that sooner or later their table of greed would tilt? She had said her goodbyes after her coffee had finished as she had a few errands to run, and she confirmed that they would see each other after his dinner. She gave him her room number, of course she would have no idea that Luke knew exactly where hers was, in fact the camera he had installed in her room gave him a perfect idea.

On his way back to his room, Luke ran into Richard, who for once looked very busy and not chatting shit like he normally did, another kind of stress seemed to have grabbed him. As he hung up his phone he worryingly looked down at it.

"What's up? You look pale and not quite...ok?" Luke asked.

"They've found body parts in the sea..." Richard replied, still looking down at his phone trying to solve the puzzle miles away from Haiti, the office and all the proof.

"Who? What body? What sea?"

Of course Luke knew exactly what Richard was talking about. His little gift to them, a little something to say thank you.

"Jack... he has been gone since our trip, and now they've found body parts in the sea in bags... Fuck, Laura is going to go crazy!"

Luke was looking around to make sure no one was near them as they were talking. "I just know it's Jack they've found... shit..."

Richard sat down on the stone wall behind him, it seemed like all the air had gone out of him.

"Hey, I mean... I don't know what has happened here or what kind of people he got himself involved with, but are you sure? Could it be someone else they've found?" Luke asked, trying to look as concerned as he could. Luke could see sweat patches under Richard's arms, the boy was crumbling too now. What beautiful sight of complete devastation happening in front of your eyes could be, Luke thought to himself. He almost wished he could bottle it up for a later occasion.

"I don't know, I guess we just have to wait..." Richard mustered up.

"Yes, try to stay calm, by the way do you think it's a good idea to start stressing Laura out if we are not even sure yet? I mean she has been so busy planning this great stay for everyone, maybe wait until you are certain and then tell her once this is over? Don't get me wrong of course you can do what you think is right, but I was just thinking, you know..." Luke said this casually as he put a hand on Richard's shoulders as if in an attempt to be a good friend.

"Yeah, you are probably right, it will absolutely devastate Laura, so I have to make sure it is him before I say anything."

Richard was clearly in shock and Luke needed him back to how he was to keep the energy at the same level. If Laura picked up this shift in Richard, she would 100% find out about Jack, and Luke could not have that happening now.

"Is there anything I can do to help?" Luke asked as he was hoping he could do anything just something to bring Richard back to how he normally was, a careless big idiot.

"No, no thanks… you've helped enough… I am going to lie down a bit and hopefully feel more positive when I wake up. Thanks, mate…"

Richard still looked out of place and time as he was walking towards his room, rubbing his head in disbelief.

Luke stood still and watched Richard walk back to the rooms. Yeah, the walls were definitely closing in now. He had a lot to do that night. Three characters to take out and he would have to be clever about it. And fast, for sure, fast. Luke decided that a bit of meditation and sleep would do him good as well, so he made his way back to his room and shut the door to the outside. It was time to take himself where he needed to be to make sure he had the best delivery of his life.

Last dinner

At around 5.00 p.m. Luke had a knock on his door and when he opened it, the masked guy was standing there with a tray, again with an envelope. This time the envelope was black. *How classic*, Luke thought to himself. Very, very original. He was happy at times when remembering mental eye rolls, otherwise he'd be fucked.

"Well fancy seeing you around here… again, what a surprise." He gave the masked guy a smile and tilted his head. Luke could feel the masked guy's uncomfortable stare, it was so easy to make people lose their shit, just by keeping the silence and staring. Simpletons.

After enduring Luke's glare for a few seconds more the masked guy nodded and made his way down the hall. Luke made sure he kept unnerving the guy to the very end by following him with his eyes until the last bend of the hallway... ahhhh, I'm gonna miss that guy... so easy to freak out not realizing that he himself was the biggest freak out of the two of them.

A sad loss of a soul, Luke thought to himself as he opened up the envelope.

Dear investor,

Please be ready for our ball tonight and a special invitation to room 616, you can find your outfit for the evening in the wardrobe.
Please do not hesitate to ask if you need anything else. We are here to please.

The Asian Orphanage.

Indeed you are... Luke thought loudly as he was tapping the invitation. He wandered off to the wardrobe to see what shit they had ready for him. Meh, your standard penguin suit... oh, I see a golden mask... interesting. Luke got himself ready, made sure he had some of his tools hidden on him, and the rest he had made sure were hidden in different places.

Let the show begin.

Room 616

Luke was on the sixth floor exactly two minutes to eight. The hall leading to room 616 was empty and quite dark. Not a very social person indeed.

As he was approaching the door, he could see three teenagers walking out of the room. They passed him with their heads down, and their shame shook Luke's core, he felt the rage kickstart. He took a deep breath and calmed himself. It would be soon, just wait.

He paced himself to the door and inhaled deeply before he knocked on the door. The silence seemed to last a lifetime.

"A minute."

Luke thought the man's voice sounded growly and old, so it couldn't be a young person he had to face.

The door opened, and inside was a waiter with a black eye mask on. Fuck was he doing there, Luke needed to find a way to get rid of him. The masked guy made a welcoming hand gesture to Luke as he stepped aside for him to enter. Luke nodded at him. It was clearly not the same loser that had visited his own room - even with silence this masked guy seem to have more oomph in him than that fucking ass.

The room was a very impressive suite. It had been set up for their dinner with everything ready.

Luke was taking in his surroundings, anything he could use for his finale, anything that could give him more details about this bastard behind all this pain and hurt. The masked man brought him a glass of champagne. Luke took it and downed it as fast as he could.

"Sorry for the delay," the man said as he walked into the room, "I'm sure you know I don't like to be late or have people being late, so this of course is a bit embarrassing. I Just had a little business to take care of…" He finally looked up from sorting out his cuffs.

Of course, he had his fucking mask on! Fuck! Luke wanted to see this man, he wanted to know who the hell he was.

"Oh no don't worry, it's ok, I've not waited long anyway."

"Great, should we sit down and start our dinner and get to know each other? I've heard…"

The man was babbling on with his pleasantries, but there was something there, Luke couldn't focus, there was something about this man that was just too familiar. Luke thought maybe it was that this man was a piece of shit and maybe that's something Luke was so very familiar with and that's why he thought of him as familiar. Other than that, there would be nothing that could bond these two men, nothing in this world.

Luke gave him a smile and "Yes, the same," hoping that this would suffice as an answer for everything he'd missed out on whilst his mind was going round in circles placing this pig.

"Please sit down."

Luke sat down. Looking at the man trying to memorize anything and everything he had on or around him. The masked man brought the starter and went back to the corner of the room. "So, tell me about yourself and how you got involved with Richard?"

Luke started to tell the story that he had made up, about being a spokesperson for a very high-status billionaire, who was looking for a new opportunity to invest, and their orphanage and another charity had got his attention and that he was exploring both.

"Oh I bet it's one of those crap charities causing so much shit for the rest of us, I mean yes they both deliver more or less the same 'Goods', but they are run by amateurs, did you see how much mess that whistleblower made? We've never had those issues with our business."

Luke pressed out a chuckle to make the guy feel more at ease.

"I hear you, from what I have seen Laura is running this ship brilliantly and Richard with his

suave charm has everyone eating from his hand, so yes you have managed to find a great team."

"Thanks, we have been working hard at this for many years, it's great to see it all come together." "It must be," Luke said with a smile and raised his glass to toast this pig's success in ruining lives. "How did you end up in this business?" Luke asked with sincere curiosity.

The man looked over Luke's shoulder and gave a little cough before he told the masked guy to leave the room and stand outside.

The man gracefully bowed and walked out.

Thank fuck.

"Sorry but I'd rather not talk about these things in front of the help, you just never know who you can trust these days," he said, waiting for the man to shut the door.

Luke smiled. "Yes, you can never be too careful."

"Well, I got introduced to this business model many, many years ago. I was in the circles of people who found these Goods interesting and then I saw with my own eyes how much my kid was making, and well it's from there really, contacts grew, opportunities grew, and here we are."

Luke felt his stomach turn. The cunt sold his own child!

"Very brave indeed," Luke said as he looked down at the meat knife in his hand. "I think I am full up now, could I please use the lavatory?" he asked, trying to keep the sick down. Once inside the toilet Luke bent down to feel his slaughter knife that he had sharpened especially for this occasion - the rest of the knives had been hidden behind the bathroom cupboard. He took out the small bottle of chloroform and the napkin, which was hidden in the same place.

He walked out as the man was pouring them another drink and walked up carefully behind him and put the napkin over his mouth, his weight dropping onto Luke. Luke didn't expect him to be that heavy. Luke dragged him to the bedroom where he could see the used sex toys and pornography playing on in silence.

Sick fuck, Luke kicked the shit around him on the floor away from him, whilst dragging the bastard to the bed.

In the middle of the bedroom was a big round bed, on the side a massage table, and next to the table were framed pictures of the cunt without a mask next to the president, ex-presidents, actors, politicians, lobbyists and in the back a photo of him and Laura in a tight embrace and kissing. The level of sickness was beyond Luke. First thing Luke needed to do was to take care of the masked asshole waiter waiting outside. Luke knew exactly how to do that the quickest with the least questions. People can't handle discomfort whether outside their comfort zone or being forced to have conversations they should not be having. He grabbed one of the dildos in his underpants, with his mask still on. He opened the door, the asshole was there, Luke noticed that the first glance had scared the waiter, as he took a little step back.

"Oh, as you can see, we have decided to take the evening somewhere else tonight, so you won't be needed anymore." Luke made sure his smile was heard through his face mask.

The man nodded and walked away.

Fucking hell, people were so easy to read and manipulate. No wonder politicians played the rest of the population like puppeteers, they were too fucking dumb to wake up and even more dumb to take a stand. Luke made his way back to the room, he made sure that he had tied the man's arms and legs, he didn't know how long or short a time he had before the chloroform stopped working. He went to get his tools which he'd hidden in the room from his previous visits, when he was setting up. The knives, ropes, he had brought everything, he didn't want to leave out anything. Luke loved to set up with classical music, a little Bach in the background, why the devil not?

Luke found the man's many passports all with different names and just when he thought he would never know this dick's real name, his knives pushed one of the frames to the floor, the picture was of the pig and Laura, sailing. Behind it, Laura had written a message:

To my love Mark, always and forever.

(More like a grandad, Luke thought to himself, he was at least twenty-five or something years older than Laura, then again, who knew age these days with everybody obsessed with perfection?)

Twenty minutes later as Luke had taken his own mask off and the pig's mask as well, he sat down and watched him come to life. He hadn't done anything to him whilst he had been asleep, Luke wanted Mark to be awake for every moment.

He started to mumble, clearly not realizing what had happened when he came around.

"Oh, Mark Hello, thank you for waking up, if you shout or do anything stupid, I will just end you now, do you understand, Mark?" Luke said calmly but extremely authoritatively.

Mark looked at Luke, first blinking, as if his eyes were still distorted from the chloroform or the alcohol or the other shit he probably had done before Luke. Then Mark tried to sit as high up as he could, taking a look at Luke, as if Luke was a ghost or something from another planet. Suddenly Mark started laughing uncontrollably, hard and loud.

Luke stared at him at first in confusion, but then the confusion slowly turned into anger, who the fuck is this psycho?

"Jason? Oh my fucking God, what the fuck! What? How did you find me? What are you up to, come on, release me now, boy!"

"You must have mistaken me for someone else, pig. My name is not Jason."

"Boy, are you crazy? I know your fucking ass anywhere, I sold it plenty of times!"

Luke's head started spinning, his eyes started rolling back and forth, his memory, what was happening to him? Who was Jason?

The Boy with the Knife

Luke crumbled to the floor. Jason! Luke! Jason... Jason... suddenly all of Luke's memory started pouring back into his mind, brain, soul and blood.

He'd turned three, his mother, his beautiful mother was there holding him, the man his face, the man in the back, his face was blurry, but he could hear his mother's voice clear as anything:

"Mark dear, get me the cake cutter please."

The music, the laughter... everything was spinning around in Luke's head. He looked in the mirror and suddenly he saw someone else, a brown-haired man, slim, tired. He tried to stand up but he couldn't, his legs were not carrying him anymore. All of this as Mark lay in the bed laughing hysterically. Luke couldn't catch his breath, the more he tried to breathe in, the more it was getting stuck in his throat. Flashback after flashback kept coming back at him like waves, he was four, men, random men came and visited, he was in rooms with them, they were touching him, putting things inside of him, making him do things he didn't want to do. And in the background was Mark taking money as Jason was in a child pose, curled up against the wall with a bleeding rectum and a bleeding heart.

He was eight, Mark was making him sit naked on men's laps, they were touching him, making him touch them, all as Mark was sitting there and watching. All through the years the memories of Mark raping him were flashing by his eyes. He was with a knife, a bloody knife in the forest, his clothes were ripped, screaming out of desperation, he was found and then nothing, all the memories switched off like a light.

Luke looked up at Mark, his father, his own blood. He took the smallest, bluntest knife he had and walked over to his bed. Mark stopped laughing and looked at Jason.

"Hello son, missed me much?"

Jason grabbed Mark's nose so he couldn't breathe, and as he opened his mouth to gasp for air, Jason grabbed his tongue and pulled it out. Mark's eyes looked like they were going to bulge out of their sockets in disbelief. Jason pulled Mark's tongue, Mark was trying in vain to make noise, but the classical music and well, having his tongue in lock made it impossible. Jason bent down, standing eyes to eyes with the man he hated the most in the world.

"Hello Father, did YOU miss me much?"

He held his tiny knife tightly and started to rub the blunt knife back and forth to cut Mark's tongue off. The blood started filling up in Mark's mouth, Jason put him on his side for him to spit it out, of course, he didn't want him to end quickly, so he shoved in a thick napkin into his mouth.

Mark didn't know what to do, he was trying to speak but of course the lack of his tongue made it a bit hard. Jason's mad laughter took over the room, Mark was scared. He finally realized that karma had caught up and it demanded payback. Jason's laughter got louder and louder as he started stabbing Mark all over his face his upper body, his head, his skull.

The knife was blunt and small enough to not make severe damage but enough to make him hurt and bleed all over. Jason didn't see Mark anymore; all he saw were all the men using him repeatedly. He walked across to the bar and brought the bottle of whiskey and poured it all over Mark's body. The mumbling scream was clouded out by Jason's laughter and the music.

The Boy with the Knife

Jason caught a glimpse of his brown hair in the window and when he turned to the mirror he saw Luke, his liberator, his other half that had kept him going. There was a knock on the door. Jason grabbed a towel and quickly cleaned his body and a robe. He looked through the door and saw Laura, perfect timing, bitch. Jason opened the door and stood to the side, Laura still standing outside called for Mark.

"Mark? Are you there? Hello?" She started to slowly walk into the room, once she was in Jason stepped forward and shut the door. Laura turned with a gasp.

"Oh my God Luke, what are you doing? Why are you dressed like that? Where is Mark? Is that a fucking knife in your hand?"

"Oh, shut the fuck up you fucking whore!"

Laura's mouth fell to the floor, she couldn't believe what she was seeing and hearing.

"You are a clever girl, so I am sure I do not need to tell you to keep your fucking mouth shut or I end you here."

Laura's eyes darted around the room trying to understand what had taken place, she then tried to get to the door and away from Jason, who now looked like a possessed person.

Jason grabbed her arm and threw her onto the floor, Laura smashed her head which made a cut and blood was pouring out all over her white tight silk dress.

"Did you really think that you were going to get away with this shit? Did you really think that you are so above everyone and everything that reality wouldn't find your ass, privileged whore?"

Jason made sure he kicked her in the stomach before he turned around to grab her hair and drag her to the bedroom. Laura attempted to scream upon which Jason again gave her a reminder kick. When Laura saw the state of Mark, she started crying and crawling her way back to him.

"Yes, that's good, crawl that way, bitch, that's where you need to be anyway," Jason said as he bent down to pick up one of the used dildos with blood on them, probably from when it was being used on one of the kids.

As Laura was trying to bring awareness to Mark, Jason threw the toy at Laura and told her to use it on Mark. Mark tried his hardest to put up what he thought was a fight, but all to no good. He was slowly bleeding to death, in and out of consciousness. Jason sat down to watch them fall to pieces, Laura on her knees, face drowned in tears and fear. She obeyed and fulfilled Jason's wish, forcing the toy into the half-dead man as Jason was laughing louder and louder.

"Please Luke please let's talk, I don't know what has happened, but we can talk about it."

Jason spat on the floor, he could barely hear Laura's begging.

"I am done talking, whore."

Jason walked over to Laura who was sobbing on the floor, he grabbed her by the hair and covered her mouth and nose with chloroform. He got the clippers he had brought and shaved all her hair off, he then put her into a huge clothes bag, and he rang for the bell boy and left the bag outside the room with a note to take it down to a car that was waiting for this bag. Jason had made sure that his friend was there to pick up this specific bag to go with a cargo shipment to China in the early hours of dawn.

His co-worker, the same person who had looked after the kids, had been instructed to undress the whore and use and abuse her at his whim. He just needed to make sure that she was in that cargo hands and feet tied and sent off to his lovely friends in the Chinese mafia, they were expecting their golden girl.

Once Laura was dealt with Jason had a shower and put his clean outfit on. He switched everything off and put the "Do not disturb" sign on the door.

He dusted himself off as he walked down to finish off the rest.

The ball

Jason walked into the ballroom, everyone was dressed up to the nines, not having any idea of what had taken place a few floors above them.

He clocked Richard from afar who gave him a smile and a raised glass. Jason smiled at him, thanking everything that tonight would be the last time he would see any of them again.

Jason had made sure that he had marked every room they kept the kids in, and as far as he knew they had not been brought out to serve for the night. He did a quick march over to the rooms which were all on one floor and guided the kids out. Outside he had a bus ready for them to take them to the nearest police station, upon which he instructed them to tell the police about what had happened to them and give evidence against each and every one of the people involved.

As he watched the bus drive away, he went back inside to finish off his business. Jason made his way to the coatroom where he had put some of the homemade bombs, he made sure he had scattered them everywhere. He started the timer, making sure he visited all ten planted bombs. He had three minutes left before they were all going to go off, and he stood there staring at their faces, taking in all of these bastards, laughing, sharing jokes, not bothered about the humans they'd destroyed in their path of greed and self-satisfaction.

He turned around to walk out.

When his uber drove away he looked back at the hotel as it blew up in the night sky, creating a beautiful chaos.

He finally felt like the spider in the web and no longer like the fly. The tables had turned.

Jason smiled to himself, he felt a peace he'd never felt before and he knew that the boy with the knife had finally been put to a restful sleep for the last time.

He looked forward to going home and finally being able to sleep.

Epilogue

Although parts of this book is based on fictional characters and events, we are all aware of the increasing problems we are facing as humans against child abuse, trafficking and kidnapping, which are growing non-stop, at an alarming rate.

It is our responsibility towards our children and every child to hold these people accountable for what they are doing. We owe it to the eight million every year to establish stronger laws and protect them. More importantly, regardless of their status or roles in we need to hold people involved in these sick trades accountable, each and every one of them.

It is estimated that nearly 800,000 children will be reported missing each year in the U.S; 40,000 children go missing each year in Brazil; 50,500 in Canada; 39,000 in France; 100,000 in Germany; and 45,000 in Mexico. An estimated 230,000 children go missing in the U.K. each year, or one child every five minutes.

In 1980, roughly 150,000 people were reported missing per year.

Now the number is 900,000. (Factretrivier.com)

An estimated 1.2 million children are affected by trafficking at any given time. Around the world, most children who are victims of trafficking are involved in forced labor.

(Save the children.org)

66% of child trafficking victims are girls. (Save the Children, 2020)

Children are also used as manpower for labor across the world. The Bureau of International Labor Affairs maintains a list of goods and products likely produced by child labor or forced labor in violation of international standards.

This list is primarily published to increase public awareness, and to encourage concerned consumers to make efforts to learn more about the supply chain and to use their purchasing power to send the message to corporations that child labor and forced labor are not condoned.

As of 2020, the list included 155 goods produced in 77 countries around the world. (IBLA, 2019)

We can and *must* all do our bit to help and protect those who need our help and protection.

It's the duty of those with a voice to speak for those who can't.

G. M

Lightning Source UK Ltd.
Milton Keynes UK
UKHW041304270622
404944UK00012B/42

9 781803 693996